THE ONLY THING I HAVE

THE ONLY THING I HAVE

stories

Rhonda Waterfall

Arsenal Pulp Press
Vancouver

ARSENAL PULP PRESS
Suite 200, 341 Water Street
Vancouver, BC
Canada V6B 1B8
arsenalpulp.com

"Little Breaks" was previously published in *Descant* #145
"Aurelia Art" was previously published as "Surgeon" in *Geist* #60
"The Film Director and the Pixie" was previously published as "Director" in *Geist* #60

This is a work of fiction. Any resemblance of characters to persons either living or deceased is purely coincidental.

The publisher gratefully acknowledges the support of the Canada Council for the Arts and the British Columbia Arts Council for its publishing program, and the Government of Canada through the Book Publishing Industry Development Program and the Government of British Columbia through the Book Publishing Tax Credit Program for its publishing activities.

Cover design and hand lettering by Nadja Penaluna
Illustrations by Sam Weber, *sampaints.com*

Printed and bound in Canada on FSC-certified paper

Library and Archives Canada Cataloguing in Publication

Waterfall, Rhonda, 1973-
          The only thing I have / Rhonda Waterfall.

ISBN 978-1-55152-293-7

          I. Title.

PS8645.A837O65 2009   C813'.6   C2009-903739-4

Mixed Sources
Product group from well-managed forests and other controlled sources
www.fsc.org Cert no. SW-COC-003438
© 1996 Forest Stewardship Council
FSC

Illusions commend themselves to us because they save us pain and allow us to enjoy pleasure instead. We must therefore accept it without complaint when they sometimes collide with a bit of reality against which they are dashed to pieces.

—*Sigmund Freud*

CONTENTS

WHEN YOU'RE GONE

Patty boards the train in Calgary on her way back home to Vancouver and takes a seat near the window. Other passengers heft their bags into the overhead storage compartments and free themselves from their winter coats, scarves, and gloves. She rests her head on the window and reminds herself of what she has been telling herself all weekend, that when she gets home she is going to tell Steve that she wants a divorce. Across the aisle, a man wearing a brown suit takes a seat and folds his jacket with two precise creases. He places the bundle on the empty seat beside him and gives it two pats, as if the jacket were a beloved dog. He opens an attaché case on his lap and pulls out a stack of papers. The train has pulled away from the terminal and snow-covered farmland moves by.

"Beautiful, isn't it," the man says.

Patty nods her head. "Yes. It is."

He tells her he is going to Vancouver for his son's wedding. Patty asks if he is a teacher and he says, of high school science. She pictures his chalk-dust mottled fingers on the breast of a young female student. She wonders if this is the type of man she will have affairs with when she has left Steve and considers suggesting they get a roomette on the train. In the same breath she knows she doesn't have the guts or even the desire for a quick tryst.

When she was a teenager she slept with any boy who touched her hair. She wished meeting people could still be that easy. When she was fifteen she met a man on the bus who said he worked for the Ministry of Health. He took her out for dinner to a place that served her margaritas even though she was underage. She let him kiss her and put his hand under her skirt but stopped him there and told him that she had to be home by eleven. Now she couldn't remember why she stopped him. Now she wished she had let him have his way with her. The science teacher clears his throat and adjusts his glasses on the bridge of his nose. What if she asked him to get a roomette?

The thought of his flesh entering her, dispersing her insides makes her tired.

The train pulls into the terminal in Vancouver and Patty grabs her suitcase from the overhead compartment and finds Steve in the terminal. He pulls his hands out of the pockets of his bomber jacket and asks how her sister is.

"Dying," Patty says and hands him the suitcase.

"That's not what I meant," Steve says.

In the car Steve turns the radio on to the hockey game. Squeegee kids attack the car at Terminal and Main. At home Patty walks past the pizza boxes on the coffee table and goes into the bedroom. She puts the suitcase on the unmade bed and picks Steve's pants off the floor. She runs a finger through dust on the windowsill and then tosses the pants into a corner and collapses on the bed.

"I can't do this," she says.

Steve appears at the doorway and asks what she's up to. Patty catches her reflection in the mirror above the dresser and is appalled by her hair and pilled sweater. When she is single she imagines she will only wear clothes made of natural fibres, no more synthetic blends. She will use only vanilla scented soaps.

"I want a divorce," she says.

Steve sits beside her on the bed. "I think you're upset about your sister. I think we should just give things some time."

"There's been plenty of time, and don't blame things on my sister."

Steve opens her suitcase and starts to unpack her clothes. "How was Calgary?" he asks.

"Cold."

"You're not leaving me," he says.

Patty walks to the waterfront; the cold air chills the tears on her cheeks. She tries to remember things her mother said or the sound of her voice but can't come up with anything. Steve's mother was what she imagined her own mother would have been like. They often went to plays or browsed through the market on Granville Island. Recipes had been exchanged. Patty follows the path along the beach. People walk their dogs, and joggers in spandex pants run by. Clouds obscure the mountains. She would move to Calgary, but all that flat land and open space made her panic; where was there to hide? Would she ever smell the ocean again? When her fingers and toes are numb with cold, she heads home.

Steve is on the couch, *The World's Worst Race Car Crashes* on the TV. Patty puts a kettle on the stove and goes to the bedroom. She finds that Steve has unpacked her suitcase and placed it under the bed. She is about to go back to the kitchen, but Steve comes into the room and pulls her to the bed. She pushes him away. He kisses her neck and says that he misses her. She tells him to stop.

"Let's have a kid," he says.

"We can't just have a kid."

Steve shrugs his shoulders and says, "Why can't we?"

"I want a dog," Patty says.

"What kind of dog do you want?"

"Are you just going to get me anything I want so I'll stay?" Patty says.

"Yes."

The kettle whistles and Patty pulls away and goes to the kitchen.

People at work are constantly asking her how her

sister is doing. She wishes she had never mentioned her sister was sick; it isn't any of their business what stage of death she's in. Patty's chest tightens. She drinks a glass of water and tries to read emails but the letters swim together. She heads outside. The sidewalks are busy with people taking early lunches. At the cocktail bar in the Georgia Hotel she orders a brandy and flips through tourism magazines. There are pictures of the Capilano Suspension Bridge, Stanley Park, and the gothic and rusted Britannia Mine. This isn't what she wants to see. Where are the beach bungalows in the Cayman Islands? Where are the pictures of escaped Canadian wives gardening their tulip patches in Holland? There are ads for Botox. Go home looking ten years younger. Is Botox a tourist destination? She finishes her drink and books a room in the hotel.

Patty mixes a whiskey and Coke from the stocked wet bar and turns on the TV. Martha Stewart cuts triangular-shaped wedges out of dough. "This is such a good thing," Martha says. After the fourth drink Patty calls room service and orders fettuccini with clams. She drops the empty miniature whiskey bottles into the garbage bin and mixes a gin and tonic. On TV a young couple on a red velvet couch declare their love for each other. They plan to get married at Disney World. The man wears a NAS-CAR T-shirt and says he knew he met the person he was going to marry when on their second date she surprised him with tickets to a Judas Priest reunion concert. The girl wipes tears from her eyes and plays with the ends of her hair.

There is a knock at the door and Patty lets the porter in with the tray of food. On the news there is an announcement of a snowstorm in Calgary. She calls her sister, but there is no answer. She mixes another drink and tries her sister again, but still there is no answer. On the Food Channel, Nigella Lawson is frying a large piece of meat in a black cast-iron pan. "This is so easy," Nigella says. Patty finishes her dinner and then flips through the menu and calls down for a banana split and chicken fingers. She mixes a vodka and orange juice. She opens the curtains and is surprised at how dark it is outside. The building she works in sits black and empty, a block away. Rain has started to fall. She tries her sister again and when she answers Patty asks her where she was.

"I was at the clinic," her sister says.

Patty mentions the news report and the snowstorm and then asks her if she remembers the song they used to sing when they were kids, with the bunny rabbit and the good fairy. Her sister says she remembers the song. Patty asks her to record herself singing it. Her sister says she will and then asks Patty again if she is all right, but Patty says she has to go because dinner is on the stove and hangs up.

A knock at the door startles Patty, and she spills alcohol on her top. She puts the glass on the side table and wipes her chest with a towel. She lets in the porter with a new tray of food. The chicken fingers are hot and greasy, and she pours Kahlua over the banana split. The phone starts to ring. On TV a woman who has had plastic surgery on her face is being introduced to her four-year-old son for the first time since being released from the hospital. Her son cries and tries to break away from her embrace. Patty answers the phone.

"I *69'd you, what are you doing at a hotel?" her sister says.

"I'm taking a break."

"Does Steve know where you are?"

"I left him," Patty says.

"Call Steve and let him know where you are."

"Okay."

"I can't die knowing you're by yourself. Steve is there to take care of you."

"Don't die," Patty says.

The line crackles and her sister tells her to call home.

On TV a couple has repainted the walls of their neighbour's house a hot pink. Chocolate bars and wine are the only items left in the mini-bar. Patty takes a bottle of red. She stumbles to the side and falls to her knees. Her vision shifts sideways and loops, and she releases the contents of her stomach onto the carpet. When the room stops spinning she gets a towel and covers the vomit. She has a shower and is wrapping a towel around her chest when there is another knock at the door.

From the hallway, Steve calls out to her. "Your sister called," he says.

Patty opens the door and lets Steve in.

A murky stain has seeped through the towel on the floor.

"Are you drunk?" he says. He takes Patty's hand and says it's time to go home.

Patty pulls her hand back, "I'm not going."

"Are you going to stay here?"

Patty pushes the food trolley against the wall and opens the window. Cool, moist air rushes in. "I'm going to Calgary," she says.

"No, you're not. You're going to come home with me." Steve pulls her to the bed. "Look at the ring on your finger," he says. He holds her left hand out. "Why do you think I gave you that?"

"So I would do your laundry?" Patty says.

"No. Because I wanted to be with you for the rest of my life."

Patty pulls her hand away and puts her hair in a ponytail.

"Now, tell me. Why are you here?" Steve says and rubs his eyes.

"I was at work and I had a panic attack. I hate our place. I hate the dust. I hate how the sun shines through the windows. I hate everything."

"We can move."

"I want to start over. I'm tired."

"Okay, you're tired. Take it easy then. We'll paint the living room. Have tinted glass installed. We'll do whatever you want."

"My sister is going to leave me."

Steve rests his cheek on her shoulder, squeezes her hand. "Let's kill ourselves. Come on, double suicide. How romantic is that?"

Patty shakes her head and cups her hand over her mouth; she cannot hide her smile.

"I guess not," Steve says. "Let's have sex then." He pulls her to him and kisses her neck.

Patty lets him push her back on the bed. His smell is a mixture of shaving cream and sweat. He touches her neck and kisses her shoulders. Patty closes her eyes.

Steve calls Patty's office in the morning and tells them she will be taking a few days off. They eat breakfast in the hotel restaurant. Patty picks at her fruit salad and chews on Steve's toast. Steve suggests they go for a drive into the Interior and find a spa to stay at for a few days.

When they are out of the city and in the mountains, Patty calls her sister.

Her sister is out of breath and says she has just come back from a walk in the snow. She tells Patty that she is going on a date. Patty asks with whom and her sister says with the guy who lives next door.

She asks Patty if she should go sans wig.

"Wear the platinum-blonde one," Patty says.

Her sister laughs and says she will.

Patty hangs up and stuffs the phone into the glove compartment. Outside snow falls and sticks to the power lines. She tells Steve to pull over. She gets out of the car and walks along the side of the road and into a field. The air feels crisp on her face and in her lungs. She collapses onto her back and sweeps her arms and legs across the snow. The indented outline of an angel forms around her. Steve falls down next to her. Snowflakes melt against their faces. They hold hands until the cold burns their fingers.

THE LAST NOTE

When Petra got home from work, she found a Post-It Note in her date book. It said, Kill David. David was in the bedroom where he had just discovered a Post-It Note stuck in the novel he was reading. It said, Kill Petra. So when Petra entered the bedroom with a gun in her hand she found David holding a gun aimed at her. Petra remembered how long it had taken them to find the right shade of taupe for the bedroom walls. David noticed that Petra's hair was lighter and straighter than usual. He wondered if she had been to the salon. They pulled the triggers at the same time and both fell dead on the new carpet.

David was at the post office when he found the Post-It Note that told him to crash his car. His palms were moist. He went out to the parking lot and ran his fingers over the red paint of the sports car he had bought in his early twenties. He revved the engine harder than usual and then drove out of the parking lot. The tires spun and sent threads of rubber and stones into the air. The palms of his hands throbbed against the steering wheel. He picked up speed and twisted the wheel. The car slid sideways. He pushed harder on the gas. Trees and houses blurred. He went through a stop sign and pumped the air with his fist. He had never felt so alive. The tires left the pavement and spun on gravel. The car hit a curb and lifted up into the air. I'm flying, David thought. The car crashed into a row of trees, the hood buckled, windshield glass shattered. David told the police that a dog had run out in front of him. He struggled to hide his delight.

Petra wiped down her desk and phone with disinfectant and then she blew out the keyboard with canned air. She put on her coat and opened her date book. One Post-It Note said, Pick up alfredo sauce and the other said, Have sex with a stranger. She wondered if David might have written the second one. She went down the street to a bar and ordered a pear cider. A gentleman in a charcoal suit sat at a table by himself. Petra picked up her drink and joined him. She stuck her Post-It Note to his hand and explained that this was what she had to do today. He dropped a fifty on the table and took her hand.

On Saturday Petra took a Post-It Note from the fridge that said, Do something new. She sat down at the kitchen table, flipped through the newspaper, and sipped her coffee. Something new, she thought, what more is there? In the travel section there were deals to Nepal and Barbados, but she had gone to both those places last year. There were cheap flights to Germany, but she was tired of countries where they didn't speak English. There were no movies she wanted to see in the entertainment section, and besides, she didn't think that seeing a movie was anything new. She found an ad for Chinese watercolour painting lessons and dialled the number and signed up. She went into the den where David had most of the wall torn down and told him about the painting class. That is new, he said.

David's Saturday Post-It Note said, Home renovation. He checked the cupboards in the kitchen for faulty hinges, he pulled drawers out and slid them back in. He went out onto the deck and stepped on boards, but none of them were in need of repair. He stopped at the wall in the den and asked Petra what she would think if the wall were two inches to the left, would it open up a whole new space? Petra agreed that moving the wall would change the room dramatically. David took out his toolbox and started to hammer away at the drywall, relieved that he now had a task.

Each morning Petra and David checked the Post-It Notes stuck to the fridge. They were divided into three categories; tasks for David, tasks for Petra, and activities and tasks for the weekend. And so they would take Post-It Notes that said things like Pick up salad fixings or Drop off dry cleaning and place them into their date books. As the tasks were completed they would crumple up the small rectangles of paper and toss them away. Petra and David liked to know what had to be done.

LITTLE BREAKS

In the Vancouver Art Gallery, Carla's clothes are too tight and the room is too hot and everyone around her is too close. At the bar she gets her third glass of wine and knows that within the hour she will have a headache. She has never been comfortable in crowds; she can't figure out what to do with her hands. The gallery is packed with people dressed in black. They roam from painting to painting and mingle in clusters.

A waiter with loose curly hair sets a tray of cheese cubes on a side table. His black shirt is tight across his chest. He takes crumpled paper napkins from the table and places them on the old cheese tray and then slips a strawberry from a fruit plate and pops it into his mouth. Carla considers asking him to dinner but knows she won't be able to muster the courage. The waiter picks up his tray of discards and walks away. The wine glass in her hand slips from her fingers and shatters on the stone floor. Wine and broken glass splash out. People nearby leap out of the way.

"Sorry, sorry," Carla says. A woman in a brown smock appears and sweeps the broken glass into a dust pan. She asks Carla if she would like another drink.

"No," Carla says. "I can't trust my hands." She wants to tell the woman that she is tired and that the wine isn't a help, but the woman has cut back through the crowd with her dustpan full of glass and wine. The waiter in the black shirt could not have been any older than twenty-three. Carla closes her eyes and presses a knuckle into her temple.

She collects her coat and goes outside. There are patches of snow on the ground. She walks until her feet ache in her high heels and her toes are numb and cramped with the cold. The Christmas lights in the trees lining the sidewalk exhaust her. A man in a black coat steps out from a doorway and, for a moment, he looks like John. She is about to say his name when the man turns and walks past her. He is not

John. She continues to walk and study the window displays in an attempt to avoid eye contact. She met John at an art auction. He arrived late and stood beside her at the rear of the room. That evening she went back to his studio and moved in two months later. He painted giant canvases without brushes; he used his hands, sticks, and, sometimes, kitchen knives, which caused fights between them on several occasions.

She bumped into John once after they broke up, at a charity gala. "I thought you hated these things," Carla said to him. "I do," he said. A girl in a teal party dress took his arm. He told Carla he was going to sail to South America. She imagines him with his canvases and paint-stained fingers on the deck of a sailboat, the girl in the teal dress lounging on the deck in a bikini. The girl would not mind the eccentricities of an aging artist.

Ahead of Carla kids gather around a man dressed as Santa Claus. He shakes hands with a young boy. She slips into a coffee shop and orders a latte and takes a seat along the front window. She tries to stop thinking about John. Santa Claus passes by the window and then enters the coffee shop. He orders a medium roast, digs through the newspapers in the recycling box, and takes a section of the *Globe and Mail*. He sits at the table next to Carla. She asks him if his beard is real.

"No," he says and goes back to reading the paper.

Carla leans forward. "Are you allowed to take it off in public?" she asks. He folds the paper and takes a drink of coffee. He tells Carla the beard has to stay on in public and that he delivers mail for Canada Post and just plays Santa for fun at Christmas. Carla asks him if he would like to come to her hotel room for a drink.

In the elevator he tells her his name is Bruce and that he used to be a counsellor at a hospital but it gave him a nervous breakdown. The hotel room is small and the windows overlook a water fountain. Carla pours rum and eggnog into two tumblers and hands one to Bruce. He asks her what she does.

"I facilitate the purchase of fine art pieces," she says.

He stirs his drink with a finger and says, "Do you like doing that?"

"Sometimes," she says.

"Do you always ask men in Santa suits to come

back to your hotel room?" he says.

Carla takes a sip of her drink and steps out of her shoes. She unbuttons her blouse. Bruce pulls his red top over his head, unhooks himself from the tummy pack, and pulls off his pants. Underneath he is wearing shorts and a Club Med T-shirt. His legs are covered in black hair. He puts the beard on a chair and asks Carla where she's from.

"Boston," Carla says and tells him she once lived in Vancouver for a number of years.

He asks her if she still knows people in Vancouver.

"No," she says and pinches the knots in her shoulders.

"Why would being a counsellor give you a breakdown?"

"I had to tell people their children were dead."

"I think sometimes I'm going to have a nervous breakdown. I suppose it's not the real thing, the full-blown deal. It's just small breakdowns. Little breaks along the way. Do you know what I mean?" Carla says.

Bruce nods his head. "I know exactly what you mean." He rests a hand on Carla's hip. She kisses his mouth and is surprised at how forcefully he pushes back. He runs a hand across her breast and slips her blouse off her shoulders. The notches of his spine under her hands make her think of a Rhodesian Ridgeback the neighbours owned when she was a child. She pulls her underwear off and lies on the bed. He pushes her skirt up over her soft stomach. When he enters her, Carla sucks in her breath and relaxes her hips, closes her eyes, and lets him cradle her. She smells fresh-cut hay. She opens her eyes and he is above her, this man she only knows as Bruce, his face scrunched up, sweat beads on his brow. Her muscles tighten; she hopes it will be over soon. Her drink abandoned on the floor at the foot of the bed.

When they are done he leans up against the head-board and wipes his face and neck on the sheets. Carla crawls across the bunched-up bedspread and grabs her drink off the floor. She wraps a sheet around her, now she doesn't want to be naked. She scavenges for her underwear. Bruce slips back into his Santa suit. She asks if he wants to grab dinner and is relieved when he says he only has the Santa suit with him and he has to get back to the depot. They are silent in the elevator but exchange cell-phone numbers in the lobby. Carla says that she is in town every few months and will give him a call, although she knows that she will never call him. They hug and he slips out the door and is gone.

When John left he said he needed air. In the weeks she stayed in the studio before she moved to a place of her own, she began to pay attention to her breathing. She would fill her lungs to the point of splitting and then exhale with a slow, drawn-out precision until she felt light-headed and had to sit down. Do I use more air than I should? she wondered. When they first met they would spend hours in his studio inventing new ways to make love. I would die if we were ever apart, he would say.

She goes back to the Art Gallery. There are only a few people left from the exhibition. Her high heels click on the floor and echo in the room. She stands in front of a large canvas with great red splashes of paint and thinks of space. The space one would need in a home to hang such a painting, the space one needs to view it properly, the space between people, between events, between the times you're happy and sad. She smoothes the sleeves of her shirt and presses her cold hand against her flushed cheek.

PAUL AND THE GIRL

Paul sat in his office long after the staff had gone home. He caught up on emails, left a few voicemails, but for most of the time, he stared out the window. He had a craving for a cigarette even though he had not inhaled smoke in any form for over ten years. He opened and closed a desk drawer that he used to store whiskey in, but which now held only files and dust. He surfed some porn on the Internet. He sighed. It was eight p.m. He turned off the computer and put on his jacket. He walked from desk to desk and studied the photographs tacked to corkboards; pictures of children blowing out candles, pictures of babies, and pictures of couples. On one of the desks there was a picture of a woman with short wavy hair. He took the photograph out of the frame and placed it in the inside pocket of his jacket and then went across the street and into a hotel bar. He took out the picture and asked the bartender if he had seen the woman in the photograph. The bartender shook his head. Paul sat down and ordered a Manhattan. A girl sat beside him on the next stool and ordered a gin and tonic. Paul took out the picture and turned it in his hands. On the back was written "Niagara with Alice." He held the picture out and turned to the girl and asked her if she had seen the woman in the picture. The girl shook her head and asked if the woman was missing. Yes, Paul said, she's been missing for over a year. What happened to her? the girl asked. Paul started to talk but then went silent and looked away. The girl placed her hand on his knee and apologized. He took a mouthful of his drink and slipped the picture back into his pocket. After a few drinks he started chatting with the girl. He found out that she had just started as an intern for a finance company. She swept her long dark hair over her shoulder and sipped her drink. Her form-fitting skirt and top did not pucker or sag. Paul leaned close to her ear and told her she was quite beautiful. She smiled and tipped her head to the side like a child. He bought her another drink. She told him stories about how she wanted to be an artist but her father made her study commerce. Paul touched her hand and told her when he was young he wanted to be a fighter pilot. Why didn't you? the girl asked. I can't remember, Paul said.

He took the girl by the hand and led her to the reception desk and told her to pretend she was his wife just for a joke. He ordered a room with a city view, saying to the woman behind the counter that his wife would not have it any other way. The girl playfully slapped Paul on the shoulder and said, Oh, Paul, you always say that.

They went upstairs and pulled back the drapes to soak in the lights of the city. Paul opened a bottle of champagne from the mini-bar and poured two glasses. He held the girl tight around the waist and kissed her on the mouth. He told her that he needed to see her naked body and she obliged by taking off her clothes. He smacked her firm bottom and put his soft penis in her mouth. After he came he rested his back against the headrest of the bed and enjoyed another glass of champagne. The girl pulled her skirt on and her eyes filled with tears. Why so flighty, Holly Go-Lightly? he asked. She combed her fingers through her hair and said, Don't call me that, that's not my name. Paul scratched at his balls and said nothing. The girl pulled her top on and slipped into her shoes. She took a package of gum from her purse and dropped a white tablet into her mouth. Do you take a lot of business trips? she asked. A few a year, Paul said. Do you ever think about dying, like in a plane or something? she asked. Paul wanted to close his eyes and go to sleep. He wanted this girl to go now. I have other things to think about, he said. She sat on the bed and rubbed her eyes. I think of dying all the time. She turned around to face Paul. He didn't respond. I see buildings falling and planes crashing, I can't get them out of my head, she said. Paul put his glass on the bedside table. We all die, he said. There must be something you think about, said the girl. Paul sat on the edge of the bed and fidgeted with the hem of the silk pillowcase. He couldn't think of anything. What about the missing woman? the girl asked. Paul went to the mini-bar and opened a bottle of rye. He tried to conjure up memories from when he was a child, he tried to remember things his father had told him, but nothing came to him. He sat on the edge of the bed and started to cry. The girl kissed his thin hair, and she too started to cry. They cried till the carpet was sodden with tears and both hoped it would not ruin their shoes.

SHOOTING THE DRIVER

We get into the cab and Darren tells the driver we want to go to the airport. I'm in the back, right behind the driver, with my hand on the gun. After a few minutes Darren tells the guy we want to get out. We pull over onto gravel that pops under the tires and stop.

"Give us all your money, fucker," Darren yells.

I bring the gun up, point the barrel at the driver's head, and yell at him to give us the cash. He reaches under his seat, the grey hair of his comb-over falling forward. His fat hands shake, and I start to get kind of freaked out, the guy's taking too long, and then there is a bang and the gun kicks back in my hands. There's blood on the window and dashboard. Darren grabs the cash box. On the radio Paul Anka sings "Lonely Boy."

We run down the alley behind the Bank of Nova Scotia and Zorba's Greek Restaurant and cross the highway. I jump over a ditch and collapse onto the ground. The tall grass hides me. Darren is bent over and hacks out a lung until he catches his breath. My guts are going to explode.

"That's fucked up," Darren says.

We walk the rest of the way to Gibb's place on the reserve and let ourselves in through the basement door. We count forty-one dollars and sixty-two cents. Darren turns on the TV. I just want to sleep.

When I wake up in the morning, I don't know where the hell I am. Then I remember I'm in Gibb's basement. Darren sleeps in an easy-chair. The house is totally quiet. Yellow insulation lines the walls between wood studs. I head down to the beach. The tide is high and there is hardly any shore, so I skip rocks for a bit and then sit on a log. Why I think of my dad, I don't know. But I remember a time I visited him when I was a kid and he was in prison at William Head. He asked me if I was taking care of Mom. I was scared and didn't know what to say.

Back at the house, Darren is still asleep. I jab him

with the toe of my boot and tell him to get up. He tells me to fuck off. I turn on the TV, sit on the couch, and light a smoke. There's nothing on but crap.

We met Gibb a few months ago at the pool hall. He invited us over and shared his beer and weed. Gibb's got to be the best fucking guy I know. We're watching some stupid twelve o'clock movie when he comes downstairs and asks us what's going on. I tell him there's been some trouble and we need to lay low for a bit. Gibb takes us upstairs and makes scrambled eggs. I'm crazy hungry and pour lots of ketchup on my eggs. Gibb puts a litre of Coke on the table. Gibb's niece hides in the hall and spies on us. When I turn around and catch her, she squeals and runs down the hall.

After breakfast, we go back downstairs and watch TV. Gibb flips from channel to channel and stops at some dating game-show. Later in the day, the back door opens and three guys step into the room. One of them wears a Raiders jersey.

"Who are the white guys?" he asks and points at Darren and me.

"Bite it," Gibb says and grabs a paper bag out of his hands.

"Asshole," the guy says, and leaves with his two buddies.

Gibb opens the bag and tosses an Oh Henry! at me. Gibb's cousin Earl comes downstairs with a case of Old Stock and hands the bottles out. Gibb starts telling us how he plans to fix some car that's been out front on blocks for years.

I'm half listening to the TV, half listening to Gibb, and thinking about ordering a pizza with the money we got when Earl says, "You guys hear about the shooting?"

"Let's get pizza," I say and put my beer down.

Gibb makes the call. Earl takes off and comes back with weed and we smoke up. When the pizza arrives we give the delivery guy a joint. He thanks us and tells us to have a good night. The pizza is inhaled and we drink more beer. Gibb asks us what we're going to do. I tell him I'm going to Sooke. I have a friend there with a cabin where I can crash for awhile.

"And do what?" Gibb says.

I don't know what I'll do, but I tell Gibb I might build a boat or something.

"My father built boats," Gibb says.

Darren sits up. "What you know about boats?"

"How hard can it be? I'll get a book or something. I'll sail to California or Mexico."

"California's nice," Earl says. "I was in California once when I was six or seven, with my pa and my sisters. We drove down in the Plymouth. Hot, that's all I remember, and my sisters puking."

Gibb asks Darren what he's going to do. Darren says he's going to Alberta to get work on the rigs. He's going to get a new truck and a Rottie pup.

"You can make money doing nothing in Alberta," Gibb says.

"You guys should come. We could all make killer cash and rent a place," Darren says.

Earl shakes his head.

Gibb takes another piece of pizza. "I'm staying right here," he says.

Later two girls stop by, and the one wearing a jean skirt sits beside me on the couch. They take beers from Earl and talk about some kid named Kevin who got busted breaking into a house and his parents sent him away up the coast to find his spirit guide. I ask the girl in the skirt what her name is.

"Virginia," she says.

I ask her if she wants to take a walk. We go down to the beach and climb on the rocks. It's too dark to see anything but house lights across the bay. Virginia tells me her dog just had puppies and asks me where I got my jean jacket. I tell her my cousin brought it for me from Vancouver.

"That's cool," she says.

We sit on the rocks and I pull her close and put my arm around her. I tell her I'm going to Sooke tomorrow and that she should come along because I have a good friend there that will let us stay with him. I tell Virginia about my plan to build a boat.

"Cool," she says.

Gibb is passed out on the floor when we get back to the house. Earl and Darren are gone. I go over to Virginia's and she shows me her bedroom, pictures of people in her family, her Grade 9 school picture. We lie down on the bed and make out. I feel up under her shirt and ask if she will give me a blow job. She shakes her head and gets off the bed. She puts a tape on and says it's a mix her cousin made for her of Led

Zeppelin and Def Leppard. I ask her to lie back down with me and she does.

"I love you," she says.

"You too," I say, and I pull her real tight to me.

She asks me where I'm from and I tell her Calgary, but I don't remember ever being there. She says she was born in a place she can't remember too, up the coast near Kitimat. I've never heard of the place but she says we can take a boat there. I say we should take the boat I'm going to build and Virginia kisses my cheek. I think of telling her about the cab driver. We lie there and listen to Led Zeppelin until we fall asleep.

In the morning Virginia puts clothing and stuff in a backpack and we head out to the road. The reserve is completely quiet, nobody's up yet.

Virginia holds tight to my arm. "I want to go to the peak before we go," she says.

She takes me back through the reserve to where the forest starts. We take a trail that climbs up the hill and opens onto a rocky area. There is an arbutus tree, and we climb onto a branch.

Virginia points at the mountains on the other side

of the bay. "That's the Malahat."

Down below are the roofs of the houses. The sky is still tinted pink. Virginia lights a smoke for me and one for herself. She asks me why I'm not going with Darren. I tell her that I don't really know him and that I don't want to go to Alberta. I want to go to Alaska and live in the bush.

On the way back to the road, we stop at Gibb's place. Darren is asleep on the couch. Gibb is snoring away on the floor. I wake Darren up and tell him I'm going. Virginia and I head to the main road and start to walk. When cars come we stick out our thumbs. Soon the rez is far behind us and the forest ends and we're surrounded by farm fields. Virginia pulls a flower from the roadside, puts it behind her ear, and starts to hum a song. I ask her what song it is, but she says she doesn't know. Right now, I don't care if a car stops. I could walk the whole way to Sooke. I tell Virginia that when we get to Sooke I'm going to take her out for dinner somewhere classy. A cop car stops behind us with reds and blues flashing. Another car pulls up and blocks us in. There is a quick yelp of siren. Cops jump out of the cars with guns pointed.

Someone yells, "Get on the ground."

Virginia takes a step back and her hands go up. I want to talk to her, but a cop knocks me to the ground. I think I hear Virginia crying. I'm pulled to my feet by the back of my shirt. The cop chucks me against the car and tells me I'm under arrest. He checks my pockets and pats me down. I tell him I don't have anything, and he tells me to shut up. He reads me my rights, and then I'm in the back of the car and the door slams shut. I kick the back of the seat and yell at the cops that they're pigs and fuck-dogs. Virginia is handcuffed and put in the other car. I call her name and smash my head against the window, leaving blood on the glass. I kick the seat again. I was going to build a boat. We were going to sail to Kitimat. The cops get in, pull the car around, and soon we are heading toward town. There is the ocean in the distance, and then we turn a corner and the ocean is gone.

AURELIA ART

In the mind of Phyllis McKay, no two people were more perfect than Aurelia and Jude Art. Phyllis noted all of their comings and goings. The lingering kisses on the front stoop in the mornings. The exotic colours that Aurelia wore, bright pinks, canary yellows. On weekends, the Arts tossed monogrammed suitcases into the back of the SUV and disappeared until Sunday night. Phyllis imagined seaside resorts, bubbling hot tubs, champagne and candles. On nights when she couldn't sleep, she wanted to creep across the street in her nightdress and watch them through the window.

One afternoon just after the Arts moved in, Aurelia Art had invited Phyllis over for coffee. Phyllis took cupcakes that she had baked herself and topped with butter icing that ran down onto the paper cups. Aurelia placed the tray of cupcakes on her granite kitchen counter and then pulled a plate of cheese and fruit from the fridge. The Arts' home was furnished in white, the floors made of rare hardwoods from the Amazon. Aurelia asked Phyllis where she liked to holiday. What do you mean? said Phyllis. You know, vacations, said Aurelia. Oh, said Phyllis, and she dropped a piece of brie into her mouth. Aurelia's chatter eddied in Phyllis's head. She tried to think of things to say in the brief moments when Aurelia stopped talking. But her mind was devoid of opinion or comment. Aurelia nibbled at her lip and stirred her spoon around in her coffee, and then she started chatting about a movie that starred street children from São Paulo.

Aurelia resembled an exotic tidal-pool creature in her brilliant orange dress and purple scarf. Phyllis searched for a scarf just like Aurelia's and found one in lime green at Sears. She tried to tie the knot so it would appear jaunty and casual. But each time it resembled a tight fist. She tossed the scarf into a drawer, where it remained as a reminder of her appalling lack of sophistication.

Phyllis waited two weeks before allowing herself to call Aurelia and invite her over for coffee. I would love to, Aurelia said, but I have French class. Phyllis suggested another time, but again Aurelia said she had already made plans.

Phyllis painted her flowered wallpaper white. She replaced the dark garments in her wardrobe with brightly coloured dresses and wraps. And then she saw an advertisement in the paper for a reconstructive surgeon and called the number.

There were rounds of operations. Cartilage and bone removed and adjusted, skin tightened and lifted, teeth capped and polished. When the bandages came off the surgeon held up a mirror. Phyllis gasped and touched her new cheekbones and her plumped lips. She looked exactly like Aurelia Art.

When Phyllis got home, she went across the street and into Aurelia's backyard and found Aurelia lounging on her patio with a gin and tonic in her hand. Aurelia shielded her eyes from the sun and said, Do I know you? It's Phyllis, Phyllis said, and she explained what she had done. Why? Aurelia asked. Because, Phyllis said. Because. Aurelia got up from the lounge chair, slipped out of her bikini, and handed it to Phyllis. Put it on, Aurelia said. Phyllis pulled off her slacks, unbuttoned her blouse, and adjusted the bikini straps on her hips and shoulders. Aurelia donned Phyllis's clothes. I'm going to go now, Aurelia said. She stepped off the patio and headed toward the back fence. Phyllis picked up the gin and tonic and sat down on the lounge chair. Aurelia opened the back gate, stepped into the lane, and began to run.

IN THE VERY NEAR FUTURE

In the bathroom, Becky untwists the neck of the coat hanger and straightens the wire and puts the hook in her mouth. She pushes until the metal digs into her throat. She gags. Her stomach muscles convulse and lock. Light flickers and fades. Her knees buckle and her forehead hits the edge of the sink. She dreams that she is on an ice floe and monkeys are chopping her into pieces. She wakes to the smell of Pine-Sol and blood. She has a shower, blow-dries her hair, puts her nicest dress on, and dabs perfume behind her ears.

The psychic's sign is lit up in pink neon. Becky opens the door. Chimes and bells tinkle.

A woman with auburn hair says, "You're in the right place." She is wearing an orange caftan. She motions for Becky to sit at a table covered with black velvet and sits across from her. "Now, dear," she says, "tell me your name and give me your hand."

"Becky." Becky holds out her hand.

"Becky, Becky," the psychic says, as if trying to stir up an old memory of a friend. She closes her eyes and caresses Becky's fingers. "Oh, yes, I see. You have many things on your mind. Too many sad, heavy things for such a girl. You have had a loss in the family recently; there has been some sickness. Oh, yes, I see it now, it's your grandfather. Did he have problems with his blood? It's something about his blood."

"He had a stroke."

"Okay, this has been holding you down, but I see happiness in the very near future. A party maybe, somebody getting a promotion, engaged. There is an invitation in the mail. It's going to change your life. I'm getting a block in your aura. There is something blocking your throat." The psychic grinds her thumb into Becky's palm. "Yes, yes, there is definitely a block in your throat. You must talk more to clear your chakra." The psychic takes her hands away and opens her eyes. "Yes, this is it, it's your throat chakra." She gets a pad of paper and pencil. "Here is a list of things you must do: burn sandalwood incense, burn this candle for one hour each evening, pour this oil into your bath, use very hot water and inhale the steam. You must root yourself. I want you to be near trees. At least once a week you must spend some time at the base of a large tree, preferably cedar, and you must get out on or near the water as much as possible. And here is a piece of rose quartz, you must carry this on you at all times."

Becky crosses her hands on her lap, leans in toward the psychic, and says in a low voice, "I think I have a baby in my throat."

The psychic sits back and rubs her chin. "Eat more cranberries," she says.

Becky cannot sleep. Outside a baby cries. She gets up and looks out the window. Headlines in the news run through her mind, baby found in garbage dump, baby abandoned in underground parking lot. She goes out to the alley and looks into dumpsters, under discarded pizza boxes, through the leaves under a magnolia tree, under the rose bushes in a brick courtyard. She steps into an alcove and the sound of the baby crying is all around her, but there is no baby. She closes her mouth and the baby's cry is muffled. She runs her hands over her neck and shoulder blades. Tears splash the dirty cement.

Roger is reading the paper by the fireplace when Becky walks into the coffee house. She orders a latte and takes it to Roger's table.

Roger puts the paper down. "So what do you want for your birthday?"

"Nothing."

"What are you talking about. You have to want to do something for your birthday. Come on, we should do something."

"Can't we just rent a video?" Becky says.

"That's lame."

"Yeah, well I'm lame."

The door to the coffee house opens and people come in with children in Halloween costumes. The children run up to the display cases and point and yell at the cakes and cookies.

The first stop at Halloween was always at her grandparents'. When they opened the door she would call out trick-or-treat, her grandma would drop a mini box of Smarties into her pillowcase and then close the door. Becky would bang her fist on the door, and when her grandma opened up again she would say, "Grandma, didn't you know it was me?"

"Who's you?"

"It's me, Becky."

"Oh my gosh. Come here, Papa, come here, this pirate says she's Becky."

Her grandfather would lean in close to her so they were nose to nose, "Are you sure you're Becky? We had an alligator come by earlier that said it was Becky."

She would fall against him and wrap her arms around his neck.

"Are you crying?" Roger says.

"No, no," Becky says, "just watching the kids in their costumes."

"Are you all right?"

"I've been feeling a little worn down. I have this lump in my throat." The coffee stings the torn flesh around her tonsils.

"Do you want anything to eat?"

"No thanks."

Roger goes to the counter and Becky reads the headline on the front page of the paper: parents make public plea for child's safe return. A little girl in a princess costume trips and falls in front of Becky. She cries out. Becky lurches forward and reaches out for her. An attractive blonde woman scoops the girl up, and Becky sits back and pushes her balled fists into her abdomen. The blonde woman wipes the girl's face with her fingers and coos into her ear. Roger sits down and places a plate with a jack-o'-lantern cookie in front of her.

"I don't want anything," Becky says.

"I know, it's just a cookie."

Becky picks up the cookie, takes a small bite, and washes it down cautiously with coffee.

"What's wrong?"

"This girl fell down in front of me and I tried to help her." Becky wipes her eyes on a napkin.

"This is why you're crying, because a kid tripped in front of you?"

"Roger, when are we going to get a place?"

"Oh, this is what this is all about."

"I want to move on with our relationship. I want a real relationship."

"We have a real relationship. Why do you have to be on such a schedule? We've only been together for a year."

"I don't have a schedule. I just thought it would be nice. That's all."

The waiting room at the clinic is crowded with people sneezing and coughing. Becky sits in the corner near the toy box and picks a book out of the box and lets it fall open. A little bird looks up at a big yellow backhoe and asks, "Are you my mother?" Becky closes the book and puts it back. In the examination room she sits on the bed and flips through a copy of *TIME* magazine. The paper sheet covering the bed crinkles beneath her. On the wall hangs a diagram of the female reproductive system. The doctor steps into the room. He shakes Becky's hand and opens the chart.

"You have a lump in your throat?"

"Yes, I have a lump in my throat, it's been there for three weeks or so. It keeps me up at night, and I can't eat."

"All right," the doctor says, "let's take a look."

Becky opens her mouth, sticks out her tongue. The doctor flashes light down her throat, then feels the glands in her neck.

"Well, I don't see anything there in the way of a lump or blockage. It does look irritated though. I'll take a swab and see what the lab thinks, but otherwise I would say just get some cough drops, and if things get worse come back."

In her mailbox, Becky finds a red envelope addressed to Mr Sierra in the apartment below her. She knocks on Mr Sierra's door and the door opens. She calls out, and when nobody answers, she steps into the apartment. On the hallway walls there are paintings of trees and ocean. She finds Mr Sierra on the living room floor. After the 9-1-1 call, the ambulance takes Mr Sierra away under a sheet, and Becky goes back to her apartment and makes a vodka and cranberry juice. She draws a bath and pours in the oil the psychic gave her and lights the sandalwood incense. She opens Mr Sierra's red envelope. Inside is an invitation to an art show on the weekend.

At the art show people are milling about with glasses of champagne in hand. For her parched throat she drinks the first glass of champagne in two mouthfuls and trades her empty glass for another full one. She stays on the outer edge of the room. The paintings are of tree roots. She studies each canvas; the thick paint casts shadows. She takes another glass of champagne from a waiter and is drawn into a conversation. A tall brunette in a black sequined dress says, "The artist and his partner recently adopted a baby from Cambodia."

Becky chews on a cough drop and thinks of the Khmer Rouge and the walls of human skulls.

"I asked him why," the brunette says, "and he said that if you don't have a child you become one yourself."

Those who have gathered around to hear nod and smile with the brunette.

Becky chokes on a cough drop and pulls at the neck of her sweater. "I have a baby in my throat," she says.

The brunette's eyes go wide. "That's not where a baby should be."

Becky finds a seat on a sofa with a view out the plate glass window at the front of the gallery. And there, walking past the gallery, is her boyfriend, Roger. His head is down and his hands are in his pockets. He is with a girl who has blonde curls that peek out from under her hat. They disappear around the corner. Becky drinks more champagne and rubs the chunk of rose quartz in her pocket. The lump in her throat feels bigger than ever.

She is getting her jacket when someone says, "Going so soon?"

She does not know him, but he has a nice smile and blue eyes.

"Maybe," she says.

Blue Eyes brings her another glass of champagne and they talk about the show and he asks her if she will come to his place for a drink. She nods and her skull feels like lead; her teeth ache. They leave together and he leads her to an unmarked door and up a narrow staircase and through another door to a large loft apartment with a rope swing in the centre of the room. Becky sits on the swing and pushes herself back.

"Girls always go straight for the swing. Guys wait till they're drunk. Why do you think that is?" he asks.

They smoke hash and drink peppermint schnapps. He tells her about his dream of being a scientist. She tells him she has a baby in her throat. He blows hash smoke into her mouth and says, "What should we do about that?"

"I think we should take it out," Becky says.

Blue Eyes runs a finger over her molars and along the inside of her cheek. "I don't see anything."

"Look harder."

He kisses her neck and runs his hand under her skirt. She pulls her sweater off and then her skirt and stockings. Blue Eyes blows hash smoke over her nipples and bites her shoulder.

Some time after they both fall asleep, Becky wakes up to the sound of a baby crying. In the washroom she blinks at her ghostly reflection in the mirror and brushes her teeth. She gargles with Listerine and then sorts through the medicine cabinet. She picks up a single razor blade. "Get out," she says and presses the sharp metal edge into the skin of her neck. Her hands shake and she puts the razor back on the shelf. On the window ledge beside the toilet there is a potted plant. She pushes a finger into the soil and then puts the finger in her mouth and sucks the soil off. She picks the pot up and scoops soil into her mouth. Grains of sand scrape her teeth. She goes to the kitchen and pours a glass of milk and washes down the last of the grit. In bed she pushes against Blue Eyes. She breathes in his scent of cologne and cigarette smoke. She collects the piece of rose quartz from her coat and holds the cool stone tight in her hand and gets back into bed. The psychic had said she would get an invitation and it would change her life.

"Are you going to change my life?" she says to Blue Eyes and moves a slip of hair away from his lax face. When she closes her eyes there is the faint cry of a baby. She grasps the quartz tighter and tries to swallow past the lump in her throat.

THE ONLY THING I HAVE

When Sasha gets into the shower, Colm goes into the kitchenette of their hotel room and pours himself a glass of red wine. He sorts through the tourism pamphlets on the counter. There are pictures of helmeted white-water rafters in inflated boats on the Cheakamus River. He tosses the pamphlets aside and pours more wine into his glass. Plush furniture fills the room, and from where he stands, the corner of the duvet-covered king-sized bed is just visible in the bedroom. Watching porn, masturbation, and sleep cross his mind. The shower shuts off and there is the dull creaking sound of the shower door opening and closing. Colm takes a mouthful of wine and visualizes Sasha in the bathroom, setting her makeup out on the counter and pulling a comb through her wet hair. Before Sasha went into the shower she asked Colm if he wanted to join her. He said no, not wanting to see her naked, wet body. The stretch marks on her hips, the cluster of acne scars on her back. When they were at the cabin in the summer, Sasha was lying on the dock, sunning herself in a bathing suit, when Colm noticed these imperfections for the first time. He wondered if she had these flaws when they met or if they had developed over the few years they had been together.

In the living room, he collapses onto the couch and wishes he could stay there all day. No phone calls from clients. No dinners to attend. And no Sasha. When the bathroom door opens, he squeezes his eyes closed and crosses his arms over his chest.

Sasha drops down onto the couch and rubs his shoulders and asks him what he wants to do. He twists his body away from her.

"Don't know," he says and tries to remember the name of a girl he dated when he was in his twenties. Her father played football in the CFL and Colm had gone over for a few BBQs. He wonders if she is still in Vancouver and resolves to find her. He thinks her name was Amy Sullivan.

"We should go for a walk around the lake," Sasha says and gets up from the couch.

He imagines having Amy over for dinner at his place and starts to doze off. Sasha shakes his arm and urges him to get off the couch.

"Come on. Let's go," she says.

He presses his face into the cushion. There is the taste of dust and perfume. "I want to stay here," he says.

Sasha touches him and asks if he's all right.

"I just want to stay here," he says.

"Why? It's nice out and if we stay inside we may as well be home."

Colm considers telling her to go by herself or that he feels sick but knows this will lead to more questions. He can't stand the questions; the constant inquiries into his state of mind and emotions. He wants her to shut up. He wants silence.

"What's up with you?" Sasha says.

"Nothing," Colm says and sits up. "Nothing's wrong." He grabs his shoes from near the door and puts them on.

They cross the village and take one of the trails that

lead to a series of golf courses and a lake. When they come across a bench, Colm sits down, pulls off a shoe, and digs a pebble out from inside the toe.

"I've worn the wrong shoes," he says. "We should head back."

"I want to see the lake," Sasha says.

"Fine," he says, angry with himself for agreeing to the walk. This has to end, he thinks and mulls over details of their relationship. They live together. He pictures the dividing of property; the fighting over furniture and CDs. Who bought the coffee maker, or was it given to them? He's sure the coffee maker came from his parents. He tries to recall what he saw in her to begin with. They met at a café where he had gone to work on his laptop, in an effort to get out of his apartment more. She was at another table reading a magazine about cars and wearing a peasant dress. The magazine was what caught his attention. Normally he hated peasant dresses on women, but found this one flattering on Sasha. Her hair was curly and looked as if it hadn't been combed. His previous girlfriends had pin-straight hair, almost always blonde. Sasha's hair was red in most light.

The trail widens and the lake opens up before them. Sasha jogs ahead and down a wooden ramp to a floating dock where someone has placed two Adirondack chairs. Colm follows.

"You're so quiet today," Sasha says and tugs on his sleeve.

There is a split second when Colm wants to hit her. The impulse startles him and he pulls away.

"Don't pull on me," he says.

"All right," she says and goes over to the far edge of the platform. She picks up a sliver of wood and tosses it into the water.

He hates the concern in her voice. He takes a seat in one of the chairs and thinks about the dinner parties he will have when Sasha is gone. He recalls a TV show he watched where a couple had gone hiking on the Oregon coast and only the boyfriend came back. A few weeks later the girl's body was found on the beach by some teenagers. They said the girl died from a fall. The boyfriend was charged and went to trial but was acquitted.

Sasha gets on her knees and leans out over the water. "There are little fish out here," she says.

"I'm going back," Colm says and heads back up the ramp.

Sasha jumps up and jogs after him. "What's going on with you?" she asks.

"I don't want to talk about it."

"Why are you being such a jerk?"

"What?"

"All week. You've been distant and snappy."

Colm turns away from her and continues up the ramp. He's tired of her voice. Sasha comes up behind him and grabs his arm.

"Get off," he says and yanks himself free from her grasp. "Leave me alone."

"You're acting like you're fifteen," she says.

Colm shoves her and she staggers back. Her arms windmill and she grabs the railing. "What the hell's wrong with you?" she shouts.

"I want out," Colm yells and heads toward the gravel trail.

"What?" Sasha says. "What do you mean?" She runs up the ramp after him and tries to hold him back. He swings around and shoves her again. This time she stumbles and falls to the ground. Colm walks off and leaves her.

In the village Colm is sure everyone is staring at him. He starts to run. His chest is tight and his breathing erratic. All he wants to do is make it back to his hotel room. Panic grows until he reaches the lobby. In the elevator he gasps for breath and holds on to the rail. When the elevator doors open, he runs down the hall, shoves the key card into the lock, and slips into the room. The door closes behind him. Colm pours a rum and Coke. He drops his head into his arms on the counter and considers driving back to Vancouver and lighting their condo on fire.

"I've fucked everything up," he says. He rifles through the kitchen drawers and grabs a steak knife. Unsure what to do, he saws the blade across his wrist, but the dull edge only creases and bruises his flesh. He hurls the knife across the room and gulps rum from the bottle. He drags himself to the couch and collapses. Then it occurs to him that he's made a mistake. He has to get Sasha back. She's the only thing I have, he thinks. He dumps his drink into the sink, brushes his teeth, and paces the room with heavy, frantic steps.

When Sasha comes in, Colm is scrubbing the kitchen counter. He rushes to her, apologizes, tells her he didn't mean to push her and clings to her.

"You've lost your mind," Sasha says and shoves

him away. She heads to the bedroom and puts her suitcase on the bed.

"Don't leave," he says.

Sasha takes a pair of pants from the floor and tosses them into the suitcase. She pushes past Colm and grabs her toiletries from the bathroom.

"Please," Colm says. "Don't go. I love you." He takes hold of her and starts to cry. "Don't leave me. I didn't mean to."

"Jesus," Sasha says and tosses her makeup bag into the suitcase. She sits on a chair in the corner of the room. "What's wrong with you?"

"I don't know," Colm says and slips to the floor. Tears streak his face. "I feel like I'm dying."

His shoulders slump forward, his eyes close. "Please don't leave me."

Sasha slides off the chair and takes Colm into her arms.

"I need you," he says.

She strokes his hair. "You hurt me."

"I'm sorry," he says. "I screwed up."

"You have to talk to me."

"I know," he says. "Why don't we get some dinner?"

When Sasha doesn't say anything, Colm thinks she must be getting ready to leave him. She stands up and goes to the washroom. Colm follows and watches her wash her face and then change into fresh clothes. He searches his mind for things to say that would convince her. She takes his hand and asks him where they are going for dinner.

He takes her to one of the most expensive restaurants in the Village. During dinner he asks about the all-girls getaway weekend she is planning to the Sunshine Coast. She tells him about the oceanside cabin where they will stay. He dislikes her girlfriends. When they come over he always remembers something he needs at Home Depot.

The waiter interrupts to ask if he would like more wine, and he realizes he hasn't heard anything Sasha has said since she started talking about the cabins. Now she is talking about some hike.

Colm interrupts her. "How long are you going for?"

"Just the long weekend."

"I don't think you should go," he says.

"What are you talking about? I have friends coming from across the country. We've been planning this for over six months."

"I think we should get married," he says.

"What?" she puts down her glass. "Really?"

"I've been thinking about it."

"It's been such a weird weekend," she says.

"You don't want to marry me?"

"It's not that," she says. "It's just you haven't been yourself lately."

"I'll be better," he says. "I promise." He takes her hand and starts to describe the setting of their wedding. How they will be on a sandy beach, the sound of the ocean. How beautiful she would look in a white dress.

"Okay," she says. "Let's get married."

They talk for a while about what kind of wedding to have. Colm wants something small, but Sasha says their families must be there. She is suggesting locations when Colm notices a couple at another table. The woman has long blonde hair and breasts that push up in a way that he assumes is surgically enhanced. He considers the idea that he needs to make more money. Women like that want men with cash. Sasha pours more wine into her glass and pushes mushrooms off her chicken with her fork.

"What about Mission Winery?" she asks.

"Why didn't you order something without mushrooms?" Colm asks.

Sasha puts her fork down. "I forgot."

When they leave there is a moment when the blonde and Sasha are standing side by side. Colm notices the weight Sasha has put on. He wonders how often the blonde works out. Maybe he'll suggest to Sasha that the gym would be a good idea. But then he realizes he doesn't care what Sasha does.

On the walk back to the hotel, Colm decides that being with Sasha is a mistake and he regrets not going back to the city. In the room she asks him if he wants to watch a movie.

"Sure," he says.

Sasha flips through the channels and calls out suggestions, none of which he wants to see. He reaches up under Sasha's shirt, cups her breast, and asks her to take off her clothes. At first Sasha pulls back, but then she kisses his neck. Her closeness sickens him and he pushes her away. Again, he tells her to take off her clothes. She stands up and for a moment does nothing. Colm considers going to the bar if this is going to be too much work but then she unzips her pants and tugs them down her legs. He grabs the digital camera from the desk beside the couch and adjusts the video setting to record.

"Don't film me," she says.

He tells her to take the rest of her clothes off.

She pulls her shirt over her head.

"Touch yourself," he says.

Her thighs fill the camera's digital screen. He focusses in on her crotch and her breasts. He sets the camera on the coffee table so that Sasha remains in the field of view, the camera silently recording. He goes to her. There is no kissing or touching. When he is inside of her, he thinks of a girl he used to sleep with and comes.

During the week that follows, Colm spends his days at work planning how to get Sasha out of his life. He hates going home, hates finding her on the couch watching *Entertainment Tonight*. Hates her wedding questions. He searches on the Internet and finds an Amy Sullivan that works for a sports marketing firm in Vancouver, and he guesses it must be his old girlfriend. He calls the number and when he has Amy on the phone he tells her it's Colm Blain. There is silence on the other end and then she repeats his name.

"We dated," Colm says. "Years ago."

"Right," she says. "Colm Blain. How are you?"

He tells her about his data processing company that he started and then asks her what she's been up to.

She tells him that she's been married for six years and that she started a sports marketing firm with her husband. They have two small children. Colm wants to hang up. He hadn't considered she might be married or have children. The thought of her children sickens him. Just to get off the phone, he suggests that if they need data processing he would be happy to quote the project. Amy thanks him and says they don't have any work for him now but might in the future.

"Sure," Colm says and hangs up.

On the way home, a car pulls in front of Colm's Navigator and cuts him off. He honks the horn and lifts a middle finger. He speeds up and rides the car's bumper. When they stop at a light, Colm jumps out of the Navigator and bangs on the window of the other car.

"Learn to drive," he yells.

The guy in the car does not acknowledge him. Colm kicks the car and slams his fist on the roof. "Fucker," he yells. The light goes green and the car speeds off and leaves Colm standing in the road. Other cars start to honk their horns at his Navigator blocking traffic.

When Colm parks in the underground at his condo, he stays in the truck for an hour. His hands on the steering wheel, he stares out the windshield at a cement wall. He pictures Sasha upstairs, waiting for him with questions about the number of guests that should be invited to the reception. He turns on the ignition, leaves the underground, and drives through the city. He needs some fresh air. After crossing the Lions Gate Bridge he gets onto the Sea-to-Sky Highway and heads north. In Squamish patches of snow start to appear at the side of the highway. He turns onto a logging road and drives until the snow becomes too deep and the truck won't go any further.

He gets out of the truck and decides to take a walk up the road for a while and maybe take some pictures. Light snow starts to fall. Colm considers turning back but decides against it even though his feet are wet. The snow gradually deepens and soon is above his knees. The sky has turned dark. He snaps a few frames of a low tree branch covered with a thick cap of snow and then continues on. The road narrows and turns into a trai; he has to bend branches back from the surrounding trees to get through. He checks his BlackBerry, finds there is no transmission, and decides to turn around. At the edge of the trail, soft snow gives way from under him and he slides into a gully. Snow plugs his sleeves and pant legs. A sharp pain stabs his leg. He drags himself under a tree and props himself against the trunk. His heart races. He makes an attempt to crawl up the slope to the trail, but skids back down. Pain shoots through his leg.

He calls the condo in the hopes that there is enough transmission and that Sasha will pick up, but there is no answer. He considers calling 9-1-1, but what would he tell them? He's not even sure where he is. Colm closes his eyes and wonders how long it would take people to find him if he died. He digs through his pockets in search of anything, maybe some gum or a half-eaten granola bar. He starts to laugh and imagines one day telling the story of how he fell in the snow and just about died. He takes pictures of his feet and the snow surrounding him. Browsing through the images on the camera, he comes across the video he took of Sasha in the hotel room. He presses play. Blurry images jump across the screen before the focus settles and Colm finds himself watching his own backside. There are glimpses of Sasha. And then he is crouched over her, pushing himself against her. Colm winces at the sight of his buttocks clenching. Sasha gazes over his shoulder, her face void of expression and her focus on the camera lens. A tight panic builds in Colm's chest. There is something about the emptiness of her gaze that makes him think he might scream. Vomit rises in his throat and he wants to smash the camera to pieces. Sasha closes her eyes and tips her head back. His attention is again drawn to the sight of his back and buttocks rhythmically grinding against her, his repulsive pale flesh. He lets go of the camera, wanting the images erased from his mind. The camera burrows into the top layer of powder leaving only the faint sound of his exertions emanating from the snow. Colm closes his eyes and wonders how long it will take.

JEDIDIAH'S WIFE

The sun was starting to set, and Jedidiah was thinking about going back to the house when he stopped the tractor and stepped carefully down onto the turned earth. His back and joints were stiff with the day's plowing. A solitary marrow squash lay on the ground. He picked up the squash and cradled it in his arms. He was surprised how well it seemed to fit, just like an infant. He pulled his woven hat from his head, wrapped it around the squash, and took it home.

He found his wife bent over in the pantry, scooping flour out of a bin and into a bowl. Kitten, he said. Kitten, I brought you something from the field. His wife grasped the pantry shelf and pushed her-

self upright. Jedidiah held out the squash swaddled in
the woven hat. What's this? she asked and took the
squash into the crook of her arm. She began to caress
its yellow skin with her swollen fingers. Jedidiah, she
said under her breath and gently touched his flannel
sleeve. She's beautiful.

Jedidiah's wife made a sling from an old cotton
sheet and nestled the marrow squash at her side. She
painted the window sills and worked in the garden.
The squash nuzzled against her. She lined a box with
blankets for a cradle.

In the middle of the night Jedidiah rolled over to
discover that his wife was not in the bed. He got up
and shuffled down the hall and found her asleep in
the rocker beside the cold fireplace with the marrow squash cradled against her chest. He touched his
wife's white hair and then rested on the sofa and fell
asleep.

When Jedidiah woke up there was the smell of coffee
in the room. He went to the kitchen where his wife
was packing homemade bread and jam into boxes
for the market. The squash lay in its cradle on the

counter. Jedidiah loaded the boxes into the truck and then went back to the kitchen. His wife, her shawl wrapped around her shoulders, plucked the marrow squash from its snuggle and held it against her shoulder. Kitten, Jedidiah asked, are you bringing the squash? His wife patted the squash on the back, held it out at arms length and said, we can't leave the darling at home.

At the market Jedidiah's wife placed the squash in a basket under the table. A woman and her young daughter came to purchase a loaf of sourdough and a jar of plum jam from Jedidiah and his wife. The daughter lifted the skirt at the edge of the table and asked, why do you have a squash in a basket? Jedidiah's wife bent down and pushed the basket closer to the girl. This isn't a squash, she replied, this is my baby. The girl scrunched her eyes and peeled back the blankets from around the head of the squash. She cooed and asked if she could hold it. Jedidiah pulled the basket away and pushed it back under the table. Stop it, Kitten, he said, people will think you're mad. Jedidiah's wife turned her back to him. He touched her shoulder, but she moved out of his reach.

That night Jedidiah's wife came to bed with the squash in her arms. Enough of this, Jedidiah said. His wife held the squash tight to her chest and said, Jedidiah, don't be cruel. See how your father speaks of you, she said to the squash. Jedidiah tossed aside the crocheted blanket, pushed himself up off the bed, and said, hand it over. His wife pulled back and clasped the squash to her chest. He grabbed at the bundle and pulled the blanket out of her arms. The squash spun in the air and landed on the floor with a thud.

Jedidiah's wife clutched the gold cross at her neck. Jedidiah seized the squash and said, this has gone too far, and left the room. His wife scooped the blanket off the floor and went to the window. Downstairs, the back door slammed shut and Jedidiah headed out across the dark yard toward the woodshed.

AROUND THE PARK

In the lounge at Bacchus, Julia leans over to the man at the next table and says, "Nice tie." He slips a business card into her hand and invites her to dinner.

They meet at Le Crocodile. Candles flicker on the tables. Afterward they drive out to the Marriott near the airport. He rests a hand on her knee. Her thoughts are many; the thrill of being with a strange man, the joyride in his BMW, the heated leather seats warming her thighs, the anticipation of sex in the air. She pictures her boyfriend, Nick, in his apartment, watching CNN on the couch. She tries to conjure up a drop of guilt for the infidelity she knows she will commit, but can't. No, she thinks, here I am, young and fresh, and this man wants a bite, and who knows where it could lead, what riches lie ahead. It is nothing but a small infidelity.

In the hotel room, they pour champagne into wine glasses. He kisses her and grabs her breast. The sex is clumsy. She turns away from his wet mouth. Sweat drips from his forehead and drops onto her collarbone. When he is spent he flops onto his back. She says she can't stay, she hasn't brought anything for the morning, and she didn't realize that all this was in his plan. He drives her back to the city. At home she has a shower and then calls Nick. They agree to meet for breakfast. She gets into bed and falls asleep and dreams of her future as she has since she was a child: What her husband will look like. How they will meet on a forest path with dry pine needles under their feet. Where they will live in a bungalow with a front door painted red.

In the morning Julia rushes off to meet Nick. She is relieved that he is unchanged, wearing baggy jeans and a fleece jacket. She embraces him, whispers I missed you into his ear. After breakfast they go to a nursery and look at plants. Julia enters the greenhouses; the air is hot and moist on her skin. She picks up a potted fern, holds it up and studies it at all angles, and then buys it. She is thrilled with this transaction, this small treat. She will take good care of this fern. They go to a movie about people who have travelled into the Amazon to share the word of God. Things go terribly wrong.

"Can you imagine being in the Amazon?" Julia says.

"Only if you were there," Nick says.

They end their day with coffee and Julia asks Nick if he will come home with her. What will we do? he asks. Julia says, relax, watch TV, or read. Nick says he feels like being alone in his own space. She begs him to come over and he says, Another night.

Julia hears the phone ring while she's in the shower. She turns the water off and wraps a towel around herself and runs to the phone. It's the BMW man. She is too busy to meet, she says, she has too many things to do. But he insists and she relents. They meet at a table in the back of a bistro known for its squash soup and crème brûlée. He reaches out to touch her, and she moves out of his reach. He lunges toward her playfully. They walk out to his car, and he suggests they go for a drive around Stanley Park. She thinks of the walk home and the high heels she has on and says fine, if he will drop her off at her place afterward. He drives into the park and pulls over where there is a clear view of the lights on the North Shore. Across the strait in the shipyards, piles of sulphur glow under floodlights. He rubs her shoulders and kisses her neck. He suggests they take a weekend away, maybe Seattle.

"What's the sulphur for?" Julia says.

"I think they make matches out of it."

She doesn't want to go away with this man. She doesn't want complications. He drives her to her apartment. They hug goodbye, and he kisses her on the cheek. She skips up the steps to her front door and does not look back.

Julia takes a week off work to visit her parents in Toronto, without Nick. Nick doesn't like lineups; he says he feels claustrophobic in crowds. She boards the plane and pulls a book out of her purse when she sits down. A man with tousled blond hair sits down beside her. Rain hits the windows. The plane accelerates down the runway, lifts off, and they rise above the clouds. The man pulls down the tray table and opens his laptop computer. The desktop picture is of two blond-haired boys with a Dalmatian dog. She asks if the boys are his.

"Yes," he says and smiles. He introduces himself as Jake and asks her if she is going home.

"No and yes," she says. "I'm going to visit my parents, but I live in Vancouver." They talk about how the cold in Vancouver chills you to the bone no matter what you wear. He says he is in real estate and that he travels a lot. He is divorced and is finding it strange getting back into dating. She wants to ask what broke up the marriage but doesn't. She hands him her business card and asks if he likes sushi.

They shake hands at the arrivals at Pearson International and Julia gets into a cab. She wipes the condensation off the window. In the back seat of a car in the next lane, a girl with a pink mitten waves at her. Julia waves back. The girl presses a naked Barbie doll to the window. The cab veers off the highway, drives past storefronts and then on to tree-lined streets, and pulls up in front of her parents' house. She gets out and helps the cab driver lift her suitcase from the trunk. Julia's mother opens the front door and steps out onto the welcome mat in her slippered feet. Julia pulls her suitcase up the steps and kisses her mom. There is dinner set on the kitchen table. Her father sits in his easy chair watching the news with a can of warm beer in his hand. Julia says hi and touches his shoulder.

"Hi, doll," he says and gets out of the chair.

They go to the kitchen and sit down to eat. Julia says the flight was fine, and it was raining in Vancouver when she left. Her father asks how the movers and shakers are doing in Vancouver.

"They're moving and shaking," Julia says.

After dinner they go to the TV room and watch the news. Snow has started to fall. Julia goes to the kitchen and calls Nick on the telephone. She is ready to cry. She wants to return to Vancouver. She gets his answering machine and hangs up. She tells her parents she is going to lie down. In her old bedroom she sits at the desk and opens a drawer. Inside is a copy of *Are You There God? It's Me, Margaret*.

The next day Julia and her mother go to the market.

They buy hot apple cider and sit at a picnic table.

Her mother points at a woman in the crowd and asks, "Isn't that Carol?"

Carol walks past with a small child holding her hand. She's pregnant. Julia drinks her cider and hopes Carol doesn't spot her. An old man with large dark knuckles plays a saxophone beside the falafel stand.

"Julia, is that you?"

"Hi, Carol. How are you?" Julia says.

"Great, just great." Carol pulls up the hand of the child at her side. "This is Christopher. So what have you been up to all these years?"

"I've been in Montreal. I'm an acrobat for Cirque du Soleil," Julia says.

Her mother makes a sucking sound with her teeth.

"How interesting," Carol says and sweeps her hand through Christopher's hair. "It was good to see you again, Julia. Sorry we can't hang out and chat more, but we're just on our way to a fair at Christopher's school." She waves and walks away. Christopher keeps turning his head and waves again just before they disappear into the crowd of people. Julia is relieved she is gone.

"What's wrong with you?" Julia's mother says and smacks her daughter's hand. "Look at that, a little one and another on the way."

Julia pushes the soles of her feet down hard against the ground and picks at her Styrofoam cup.

"Didn't she graduate with you?" her mother says.

"No, she caught a bad case of venereal warts in our senior year and had to stay back because she spent so much time in the hospital."

"Oh," her mother says.

When they get back to the house, Julia goes out to the yard where her father is nailing a new board on the fence. He stops banging and takes a drag off the cigarette hanging from his mouth.

"How is Mick?" he says.

"It's Nick, and he's fine," she says.

She is in her old room when her cell phone rings. The number displays a Toronto area code. She picks it up and it's Jake, from the plane. He asks if she is free for dinner. She tells her parents she has a work associate in town and meets Jake at a lounge where they play incoherent music. They drink gin and tonics, and he tells her about the projects he has been involved with in the Okanagan and in Whistler, a few in Alberta. He talks about his boys. He tells her about the city house he has just bought and is renovating. The bar is crowded with people in their midtwenties. They hold blue and green drinks that glow under the lights. She wonders if it's raining in Vancouver. She wonders what Nick is doing. Julia tells Jake that she hasn't been feeling well lately. He suggests time off.

"That's what I'm doing right now," she says, but Jake interrupts her and starts to talk about his workout routine and then some ski trip with his sons. She nods her head and tries to think up questions about skiing. He asks her if she wants to see his place.

They walk three blocks to his home. Inside he touches a control panel on the wall and a gas fireplace sparks to life. He rushes off to the kitchen and brings back a bottle of wine and two glasses. There is no furniture, so they sit on the floor in front of the fireplace. She wonders how he can live in an empty place. She sips her wine and knows it will mix poorly with the gin she has already consumed. He starts to rub her feet. She wishes she could call Nick and hear his voice right now. Jake kisses her.

Julia tucks her feet back under her and says, "I have to go." She puts her jacket on and leaves. The streets are empty. She pulls out her cell phone and calls Nick. She tells him that her parents are driving her nuts. Then she asks him if he really loves her. He says of course he does and asks if she has been drinking. He tells her to get some rest. Julia wipes away tears and says all right and hangs up. She hails a cab and when she gets back to her parents' all the lights are out. In her old bedroom she gets undressed and slips under the covers. Her mother knocks on the door and asks her if she is all right.

"Yes, mother, I'm fine," she says.

Over the next few days, Julia stays close to the house. The thought of going out and having to talk to people pains her. She bakes banana bread and oatmeal cookies. When it's time to call a cab for the airport, she leaves Tupperware containers full of cookies and squares on the kitchen counter. She knows her parents will never eat them. She calls Nick before boarding the plane. He agrees to pick her up at the airport in Vancouver. During the flight Julia gets up several times and wanders up and down the aisle. The movie is a bad comedy that she stops watching after ten minutes. She tries to distract herself with the two issues of *InStyle* magazine that she brought, but it's not enough. She daydreams about what the people on the ground are doing. She thinks about leaving Nick. She imagines the plane crashing into the ground or into buildings.

She embraces Nick at the arrivals gate, and they get her baggage and then go for lunch at a diner. Julia puts a quarter in the tabletop jukebox and hits a button and soon Elvis is singing.

"I have something to tell you," Nick says.

Outside a mother pulls at the arm of a small boy. She grabs his shoulders and shakes him till he starts to cry. As he climbs into the back seat of a car, the mother hits him on the back of the head.

"What is it?" Julia says.

"I'm going to a Buddhist retreat in the Yukon for a year."

Julia's eyes go wide, and she gets out of the booth. "You're an idiot," she says and leaves the diner. Outside she realizes her luggage is in Nick's trunk, and she is too far away from anything to walk. She pulls out her cell phone and calls a taxi.

Nick follows her out to the parking lot. "Talk to me," he says.

"You're running off to the Arctic."

"The Yukon," Nick says.

"Whatever. I want my luggage."

Nick opens the trunk, and Julia pulls her suitcase out.

"Don't do this, Julia. Why don't you just let me take you home?"

"Screw off," Julia says and pulls her suitcase to the curb. When the taxi shows up, she gets in and calls the BMW man. He is thrilled to hear from her and gives her his address. When she arrives he makes a comment about her suitcase, but she ignores what he says and starts to kiss him. He pushes her up against a hallway table and is inside her and has climaxed before she has taken her jacket off. She doesn't want to be here with this man as he tucks his wet dick into his pants. She wishes she had asked the taxi to wait outside. He asks her if she would like a drink and then jokes that usually the drink comes first. She sits on a stool in the kitchen while he pours her a rum and Coke. The kitchen is decorated in oranges and browns. She tries to imagine what she expected his place to look like but can't think of anything. She has another drink and says she has to go. He offers to give her a ride home, but she insists on a taxi. She wants to get away from him. There are no pictures on the walls.

"Do you have children?" she asks.

"No, never quite got around to it."

The taxi pulls up and she grabs her suitcase and rushes to the door. She ducks his embrace and waves as she runs down the front walk.

"I'll call you," he yells.

She gets in the cab and gives the driver her address. It is dark when the taxi pulls up in front of her apartment. She erases the messages that Nick has left on her phone without listening to them.

Weeks pass by. Julia is at work, reading emails at her desk. Down the hall in the accounting department, a birthday is being celebrated. Julia turns her computer off and sits back in the chair. She wants to call somebody, tell them she will be late; there is a party. But who would she call? She walks down the hall and someone hands her a drink as soon as she enters the room full of co-workers. She gulps down the first drink and takes another and a napkin full of crackers and cheese from a platter. Stu from accounting sits near the window with a plastic cup in his hand that he keeps squeezing. His thick brown hair hangs over his eyes.

"Are you having a good time?" Julia asks.

"Okay," Stu says. "And you?"

"I would rather have my eyes pecked out by crows."

Stu squeezes his cup and drinks the last of the pale liquid. He puts the cup under his chair and wipes his palms on his corduroy slacks. "I think I need some fresh air. How about you?"

Julia and Stu walk down Howe Street to the waterfront. The sidewalks are slick. The harbour is quiet and clouds hang low and dark. They sit on a bench. Seagulls with outstretched wings drift in the air. Julia has heard a rumour that Stu's wife left him two years ago after their daughter died of meningitis at the age of nine. Julia asks if he thinks his wife will come back, and he says no. They walk along the seawall and go to the parkade and sit in Stu's car. He rubs his eyes and rests his hands on the steering wheel. Julia leans over and kisses him on the cheek. He pushes her coat off her shoulders and runs his hands under her shirt. His cold hands on her warm chest. She sucks in her breath and tugs at the small metal toggle on the zipper of his pants.

"I watch you in the office," he says and presses into her, frantically shifting the layers of winter clothing. Condensation builds on the windows. When they are finished he rests his head on her chest. Tears slide down his face and dampen Julia's shirt.

"I miss her," he says.

She does not ask which "her" he is referring to. They sort out their clothes. Stu starts the car and Julia gives him directions to her apartment. They are quiet on the drive through the city. Stu pulls up in front of Julia's apartment building, and they embrace before she gets out of the car. In her mailbox she finds a postcard from Nick with a picture of a dog-sled team on the front. In his pinched handwriting he says he is sorry things ended the way they did and that he has found great peace at the retreat. The northern lights are inspiring. She rips the card in half and lets the pieces fall to the ground. Stu is still sitting in his car, watching. She asks him to come in. Inside the apartment Julia grinds coffee beans and boils water. They sit in the living room and talk. Julia points out family members in the photos on the mantel. Stu asks what it was like being an only child.

"Quiet," she says.

Stu tells her he always wanted a big family. Julia asks him to spend the night. They get undressed and slip into bed with the lights off. Stu kisses her shoulder and dabbles his fingers along her spine. The sex is slow and passes without comment. Julia opens her eyes, sure that he is crying. In the dark she can't tell. They lie without touching and fall asleep.

Julia wakes in the night. She is startled by the body beside her and then remembers Stu. His face slack and his lips parted. She decides that tomorrow she will ask Stu to move in with her. Tomorrow she will have a shower and make poached eggs and coffee for his breakfast.

FOUND

A fierce wind whipped through the city streets and lifted Myrna's skirt. Construction men sitting on a cement retaining wall pointed and laughed at her. She pushed down the billowing pleats and cinched them tight around her knees. The lesson book in the crook of her arm hit the sidewalk and unleashed a flurry of sheet music. She rushed to gather up the papers, but the wind snatched them away. Fiddlesticks, she said, and sat down in a doorway. Plastic bags and other flotsam swirled in the gutters, hanging signs snapped back and forth against their hinges. I never wanted to play piano anyway, she said. Wind buffeted the street lamp in front of her. Metal rivets creaked and moaned. Myrna got up and put her ear to the post. Yes, did you say something? she asked.

The post was silent. The street lamps flickered and then snapped on. She wrapped her arms around the post and hugged it tight. The metal was cold on her cheek. The construction men threw their half-eaten sandwiches at her and called her crazy. She ran all the way home.

Her mother sat at the kitchen table with a Newport alight between her bony fingers, a mint julep and a *Chatelaine* magazine before her on the table. Her glassy eyes swivelled up to greet Myrna. How was piano, dear? I didn't go, Myrna said. That's nice, dear, her mother said. She flipped a page of her magazine and took a drag of her cigarette. Your father is out fixing the car. Myrna went to the window. A Lincoln Town Car sat in the driveway with four flat tires; weeds had grown up through the engine block. Myrna poured herself a glass of water and went upstairs to her bedroom. She opened the window and got into bed. The curtains ballooned out and swished around the sides of the window.

In the night Myrna sat up in bed unsure of what had caused her to awaken. She cupped her hand at her ear and heard someone say her name. She got out of bed and went to the window. The wind had uprooted trees; they lay on their sides with their dirty roots pulled from the earth. Shingles broke away from the roof and clacked down on the street below. She heard her name again. She went down to the street and followed the sound of her name back to the street lamp. The street lamp shook and rattled. Myrna placed her ear to the metal post and was again sure she heard her name. Her hair whipped against her face and stung her eyes. She parted her lips to say Dad, but the wind filled her mouth and stole the word away. She slid down to her knees and eventually fell asleep.

Just before the sun was up a man in a flannel checked shirt bent down and touched Myrna's cheek. Rise and shine, little bird, he said. Myrna opened her eyes and thought at first that her father was kneeling at her side but then realized he was a complete stranger. She sat up and pulled away from him. I would never hurt you, he said and then explained that he worked at the construction site across the street. He took her out for eggs and bacon and then took her home to his bungalow on the edge of the city. In the corner of the sitting room he had a piano that over the years

Myrna gladly plunked away on for his enjoyment. He would smoke his pipe, and after every song hold her in his arms and say, I always knew I would find you. And Myrna would say, I searched for you everywhere. The smell of sawdust in his hair was familiar to Myrna and filled her with warmth and nostalgia, although she never knew why.

FOR YOU, BUNNY

"Do you think my wife is hot?"

This is what the guy asks me, the guy who showed up at the party driving an Audi TT. How his wife got to the party I'm not sure, because I don't remember her getting out of the car. Now she's sitting on the couch, wearing shorts, and I have to agree she is undeniably hot.

"Yeah," I say to the guy, figuring he invited the answer. What do you say to a guy who asks if his wife is hot? You can't tell him he married a dog. Not that this is the case; she is no dog. He nods his head, I guess, pleased with the answer.

"Want to sleep with her?" he says.

Sleep with her, Christ, I don't know. Who asks if you want to sleep with his wife? It crosses my mind that this is some kind of setup. Like he's going to kick my head in if I say yes. His wife uncrosses her legs, and for a split second her shorts gape at the thigh, and there is a flash of underwear. Her feet are bare. I know chicks think guys are just after their tits, but that's not always the case. I like ankles. Last year, on my nineteenth birthday, we went to see strippers. When the first show ended and the chick was gathering her stuff, I was kind of surprised it was over. I asked my friend if that's all there was and he asked me what more I wanted. What I wanted was for her to take off her boots. Every girl did the same thing, got naked but kept her boots on. Major disappointment.

The guy is still looking at me and casually drinking his beer. Like he just asked me what my favourite TV show is or something, not if I wanted to bang his wife.

"Sure," I say.

He nods his head again, takes a drink of his beer and then walks away. Leaving me to wonder what the hell that was all about. I take myself and my beer out to the backyard. A bunch of people are sitting around in lawn chairs, and I get chatting with my buddy Eric about the weekend we have planned wakeboarding in Kelowna. It's a perfect evening. The sun is setting and the air is still warm. There's even the smell of someone cutting their lawn. It couldn't get any better. Eric takes off and I gaze at the fence, lost in my thoughts. My brain feels fuzzy from the beer. That guy's wife sits in the lawn chair beside me.

"Hey," she says.

"Hey," I say back and take a quick scan of the yard for her husband. She asks me how I know the guy who's holding the party. I tell her that I don't know him that well. He's actually better friends with my buddy Eric from BCIT.

"Are you still in school?" she says.

"One more year," I tell her. "And I'll have my electrician's ticket."

"That's great," she says. "Electricians do well."

"Yeah, I guess," I say and take another scan of the yard for her husband.

"We were wondering if you would come home with us," she says.

For what? I want to ask, but I have a pretty good idea what they want, or at least I think I do. "Where do you live?" I ask, like it really matters.

"Not far from here," she says and introduces herself as Karen.

And then there I am in her car heading back to

their place. The driveway we pull into actually has a
metal gate. The gate's open, so it's not like it's keep-
ing anyone out, but it sends a message; there's expensive shit in this house. We park in the garage. She
leads me into the house and we head down a corridor
that opens up into a kitchen.

A girl younger than me comes around the corner. At first I think she's their daughter, but it turns
out she's the babysitter. Karen gives her some cash,
and I notice she checks me out. Her grin makes me
think she knows what I'm there for. The girl takes
her money, and Karen disappears with her for a bit.
I hang in the kitchen and check out their cool shit.
Karen comes back and catches me looking in the
fridge.

"Are you hungry?" she says.

"No," I say. "I've just never seen a fridge that big."

There's a moment where we are quiet and just
looking at each other. I try to suss how old she might
be. But I'm bad with shit like that. She could be
twenty-two or 102 for all I know. Her skin, though,
is perfect, smooth and tanned.

"You have kids?" I ask.

"Two," she says. "They're sleeping downstairs,
they won't hear us."

She doesn't look mom-like. At least not like my mom, thank God. Right then a soft look comes over her face, and I get ballsy and kiss her. Right away I want more. She pushes me back and asks me what I'm doing. I find it a strange question because I thought I was doing exactly what she wanted. I don't answer her and she doesn't ask for any more of an explanation. But there's something weird about the look on her face like I just killed her puppy or something. Come on, she says, and I follow her upstairs. We go into a bedroom and then a smaller room like a living room with couches. Her husband is there, standing at a cabinet making a drink. Karen and I sit on the couch. Her husband asks me if I like gin, and I say yes even thought I don't. When he hands me the drink a rush goes through my body and I think of leaving. Just standing up and announcing that I've changed my mind and getting the hell out of there. If it was only Karen I wouldn't be freaking, but the husband, what is he going to do? He sits in a chair across from us.

"Have you been with many girls?" Karen says.

"Sure," I say. Six, I think. I don't know if that's many or not.

"Touch me," she says.

"Where?" I ask. Why, I don't know.

"Wherever you want," her husband says.

The sound of his voice grates on me. I don't want to be reminded that he's there. I touch her leg, the inside of her thigh where the skin gets soft. I run my hand up till I meet the hem of her shorts and slip my fingers underneath and feel for her underwear. She closes her eyes. I wonder if the husband is going to say anything or order me to do something, but he doesn't. I push her legs open and get down on my knees and start to kiss her thigh. She smells great. Now I just want to fuck her. No show, just screw her brains out.

"What are you doing?" she asks.

"What?" I ask. "I'm kissing your leg. Is that okay?"

"Sure," she says. "It wasn't what I was expecting."

"Am I not doing this right?" I ask.

"Sorry," she says and tells me to continue.

I glance back at her husband. His position and facial expression haven't changed one iota. I turn back to Karen and for a moment think about leaving again. I lift up the bottom of her shirt, and her hand shoots out and stops me.

"What now?" I ask.

"I don't like my stomach," she says.

"I don't care," I say and pull her shirt up. There's nothing wrong with her stomach; it's flat with stretch marks. I guess it's the marks she's freaking about. I can tell she's uncomfortable. She doesn't want me to see her stomach, and there's something about that I like. I press hard against her and kiss her neck, pinning her to the couch. My hands on her chest. Now I know what I want and get her down on the floor and start taking off her clothes. As soon as I am inside her, all I think about is not jizzing. And then there is a hand on my shoulder and her husband is pulling me off. I try to fight him, but he's a hell of a lot stronger than I am.

"Bugger off," he says and gives me one last shove.

I fall back, my shoulder hitting the wall. By the time I gain my balance he's already making it with his wife.

Fuck him, I think. Douche. I want to knock him out. I'm totally pissed, and I want to see Karen's face. I want to see her expression.

"Fuck this," I say and grab my pants and knock a glass of gin over onto their stupid carpet. Before I leave I hear him ask her if she likes getting it from other guys. I'm gone before she answers. I head down the stairs and spend a moment in their living room. They have a killer flat-screen TV. It must be worth a fortune. When I get outside I'm not even sure where the hell I am, and it's cold. I walk until things start to look familiar. Finally a cab drives by. I wave it down and go home.

When I wake up, I don't know if the whole Karen thing was real. I call my buddy Eric and tell him what went down.

"That's messed up," he says. "Was she nasty?"

"No," I say. "She was nice."

"What you going to do?" he asks.

"I don't know," I say, but I do know I have to see her again. The only problem is finding her. I probably couldn't find her house. She mentioned she worked at some design school, interior design or something. I Google design schools in Vancouver and get a few choices. I check out their staff lists and come across a Karen Holmes. I call the phone number and get an answering machine, but the voice is Karen's. She says they're out for the summer but leaves a phone number for emergencies. I call the emergency number and she answers.

"Karen," I say. "It's Steve from last night."

There is no response on the other end and, for a moment, I think she's hung up.

"I want to see you again," I say.

"I don't think that would be a good idea."

"I want to see you without your husband."

"Listen," she says. "I can't talk now. I got the kids and we're in the market. I'll give you a call later tonight or tomorrow."

"Really?" I ask.

"Yes, really," she says.

I'm sure I'll never hear from her again. I go to work and otherwise just hang out until she calls a few days later.

"Can I see you tonight?" I ask.

"If I can come over to your place."

I've never cleaned so bloody fast. I pick all the crap off the floor. Shoes, clothes, CDs. I spray Febreze on everything. When she arrives the place smells relatively decent. I can tell she is wary when she walks in, looking about like something is going to jump out and bite her.

"Where are the kids?" I ask. I don't know why I ask, like I expect them to come wobbling up behind her.

"They're at their grandparents'."

She is smaller than I remember her, petite. She leans against the arm of the couch and asks me what I'm looking for.

"I don't know," I say. "I want to see you."

"What kind of see?" she asks.

"You know, like we see each other every once in a while." I sweep the hair from her shoulder and kiss her.

"Stop pawing me," she says.

I take hold of her waist, pull her to me, and force a kiss out of her. I back her up to the box spring and mattress I have on the floor and get her to lie down and unbutton her shirt and take off my pants. I press my face into the hollow of her neck, my fingers inside her. I ask her if it feels okay, but she doesn't answer. She lets me slip myself inside of her, and I want her to stay all night. When I am done I hold her tight. I kiss her neck.

"I want to see you," I say.

She doesn't say anything.

"Hey, I'm talking to you," I say.

"I don't want to talk," she says. "I talk all day."

"You just want to lie here?"

"Yes," she says.

So that's what we do, and we fall asleep. I wake with a jolt because she's up and trying to get her clothes on as fast as she can and cursing.

"I have to go," she says. "I have to pick the kids up."

"How old are they?" I ask.

"Eight and six." She runs to the door, but I beat her there and demand a kiss before she goes. She kisses me on the cheek. I tell her that I'm going to Kelowna on the weekend so I won't be around, but I will be thinking of her.

"That's sweet," she says and leaves.

Kelowna is completely stoked. We rent a houseboat with ten friends. I wakeboard all day and drink all night. I love Kelowna and would move here in a heartbeat. There's even this sweet honey, Amanda, who keeps hanging around me. She's real tight. Blonde hair. She doesn't wakeboard, but when I get back to the houseboat she says that she saw me out there, and I looked totally pro. She asks me if I have a girlfriend, and I tell her I have a girl in Vancouver. Too bad, she says, I think I could be better. I don't think you could, I tell her. She looks hurt and spends the rest of the night sulking with her girlfriends. I try to call Karen's cell late that night. She doesn't answer, but I leave her a message, telling her how much I miss her. I tell her she's my bunny.

My first priority when I get back is to have Karen, and soon enough she is back in my apartment and we are back in bed. I ask her what her kids' names are. Jillian and Cooper. I ask her if I can meet them, and she says no. We start to meet at my place every Tuesday night. Her husband has some course that night and she can leave the kids with her parents. Sometimes we see each other on the weekend, a few times back at her place. I ask her every Tuesday, will I see you on the weekend? It's always a maybe. Sometimes I see her, sometimes I don't. I ask her if she has been with any other guys, like how she met me. She says no, but it's hard to tell if she is lying. She doesn't answer most of my questions. When I'm not with her I try not to think about her but I always do. Sometimes I call her house. If she answers I ask if her husband is home. If he's there she will say something like, "Sorry, don't want any," and hang up. If he isn't home she will tell me to stop calling her home number. I ask if I can see her. Sometimes it works. Once her husband answered, and I pretended to be calling from the *Vancouver Sun* and asked if he wanted the paper delivered.

Karen is in my bed and mentions she is taking the kids to Kits Pool the next day. I ask her if I can come, and she says no, but later she says that I can be there as long as it doesn't look like I am with them. I go to the pool early and camp with my towel on the grass. Around 1:30 she arrives with the kids. She sets out a blanket and pulls out bags of carrot sticks. I move my towel closer to her blanket. She acts like she doesn't notice me, but I know she knows I am here. She rubs the kids down with sunscreen and pushes orange-coloured waterwings onto the boy's arms. The kids run off toward the pool. They both clown around at the edge of the pool, dipping in their toes and screaming that the water's freezing. I wonder what it would be like if they were my own, if I was their father.

"I love your children," I say to Karen. She ignores me. I lay back happy to have the warm sun on my skin and be there with Karen. She pulls out a novel and starts to read. Once in a while I glance over at her. She wears a turquoise bathing suit. I imagine her naked. When the kids come back, they are wet and squealing that they are hungry. She digs into a bag and pulls out potato chips. The kids stuff chips into their mouths and then run off again.

"Do you want some chips?" she says.

"My mom told me not to take chips from strangers."

She almost laughs. I've never seen her full-out laugh so this little bit really thrills me. She tosses a bag of chips at me and goes back to reading her novel. In a while she starts packing up all their stuff.

"Hey," I say. "You can't leave without giving me a kiss."

"We had a deal," she says.

"Screw the deal," I say. I get up and grab her wrist. "I want a kiss before you go."

She glances over at the pool. The kids splash around. I take her behind the concession stand and kiss her long and hard. I can feel her squirming, trying to get away, but this time I'm not letting her.

I try to ask Karen questions about her job, but she never tells me anything. I ask her questions about her husband, too. How often he's away or if he's a good father to her children, if she will leave him. She tells me that these are things I don't need to worry about. But that pisses me off. I want to worry about these things. I want to worry about her. She tells me she won't be able to see me next Tuesday because she has some dinner she has to go to with her husband. Sounds stupid, I guess, but I'm angry that she's going out with the creep she's married to. I get her to tell me where they're going. Some swish place in Yaletown. I call Karen a few times and try to talk her out of going to dinner. She stops answering her phone. I head down to the restaurant and wait for them behind a dumpster. The Audi pulls up and the valet guy grabs the keys from Karen's husband. He's wearing a grey suit. Karen gets out of the car and she looks drop-dead, mint. She's wearing a strapless dress in green. I text her, you look choice, bunny. I want to see her expression when she gets the text, but she's in the restaurant before the message transfers. I think of sticking around until they leave, but who knows when that will be. I decide to go home and play some Xbox.

How can I make her leave her husband? I write a list of all the reasons she should leave him. He's a jerk and a creep. He's away a lot. And that's about all I come up with. I make a list of why she should be with me. I'm not a jerk. I don't travel. I would be good with her kids. I love her.

When she calls the next day, she tells me I shouldn't text her. She asks if I was at the restaurant. I tell her I waited outside and she asks me not to do that. I ask if I can see her and she says she will be over that evening. I decide to get flowers at the corner store down the street that has buckets out front with bouquets wrapped in shiny foil. I pick out some that don't look too beaten down.

I sit around my apartment until ten, but she doesn't show. I call her cell and don't get an answer. I'm pissed off and head out on my bike to her house and bang on the door. Inside a dog starts to bark. I step back for a moment and check out the front of the house again because I can't remember them having a dog. A woman who is as old as my grandmother opens the door, and a small puffball of a dog leaps about at her ankles.

"Yes?" she asks.

I open my mouth and for a moment don't know what to say. "Is Karen here?"

Karen appears and tells the old woman that I'm a paper boy come to collect a cheque. The old woman nods her head and fades back into the house. The small dog follows her.

"What the hell are you doing here?"

Her anger totally takes me off guard. "We were supposed to hook up."

"Something came up," she says and tells me to leave.

I start to bitch but she tells me to back up, turn around, and go. On my way home I tell myself that it's over, she's too much hassle. I should have hooked up with that honey in Kelowna.

The next morning, she appears at my door and tells me her father had a heart attack and that's why she couldn't come over or talk. I feel like a total ass. We watch TV for a bit and then she announces that she should go. I ask her not to, but she says her mom's at her place and everyone is freaking out and her husband is in town. When she's at the door I remember the flowers and ask her to hold on for a moment. I run to the fridge and bring out the bouquet and hand them to her.

"What are these for?" she says.

"For you, Bunny," I say.

"Why?"

"Because I thought it would be nice."

"Oh," she says and hands them back. "I can't take them home."

"Keep them in your car."

"I'll keep them here," she says and comes back into the apartment. She fills a large glass with water and puts them on the table and then leaves.

The next time Karen shows up, she wants to go for a drive. We head out past the university and pull over near a park and make out. I ask her why we are in a park, and she says she just felt like getting out. We make out for a bit, and then she pulls her panties down and gets on top of me. I push my face into her breasts.

"I love you, Bunny," I say. When she doesn't respond I say it louder. "I love you." I grab her shoulders and shake her until she opens her eyes. "Look at me," I say.

"What?" she says.

"I just said I love you."

"I heard you," she says.

Her attention is taken by something behind the car. I look back and see what I am sure is the grey back panel of her husband's Audi.

"Was that your husband?"

She kisses me on the mouth. "No," she says. "It was some other car."

When she drives me home she doesn't come in. I ask her to but she says she has to get home. As soon as I get in the apartment, I call her on her cell and ask if we can take the kids to the pool again, like we did last time.

She laughs. "We didn't take the kids to the pool. I did. You just happened to be there."

"Well, maybe this time, we can do it. You and me together."

"Maybe," she says.

I've asked Karen several times if she will leave her husband, and she always says no. When I push her and ask why, she says it would be too complicated and they have children. I tell her I would take care of them all. The first time she laughed.

"Where? In your apartment?" she says.

She could tell she hurt me. She even said sorry and

gave me a blow job. I ask her if her husband knows she cheats, and she says of course not. I ask her if her husband cheats on her and she says probably.

I start to find out as much as I can about her husband, who works in a tower downtown. On a few occasions I wait at the main doors hoping maybe I would see him come out, but I never do. I decide to go up to his office. The elevator opens right across from the reception desk. The girl asks if she can help me. I ask if there is a Dean Holmes who works here; there is, but he is in a meeting. I ask if I can get his card and she hands one over. When I get back to my bike, I call the number on the card. He answers and I hang up.

I get a call from Karen saying she's going to the beach with the kids and that it would be okay if I show up like last time. I decide to get the kids a gift. At Canadian Tire there are plastic shovels, buckets, and badminton sets. I decide to get them an inflatable mattress. At home I blow the mattress up so the kids won't have to. It takes me an hour and I feel light headed when I'm done. With the mattress pinched under my arm, I get on my bike and head to the beach. I park near the concession stand and head out toward the water. I spot Cooper first. He runs out to the edge of the surf and then back toward Karen. Karen stands up and I notice there is someone with her. It's her husband and he looks right at me. I head back to my bike. I feel like I'm going to cry. I shove the mattress into the garbage bin. Shove it in till it's all folded over on itself and then ride home. I get a call from Karen that night. Sorry is all she says.

I find out where Karen's husband parks and wait for him to come out and get in his car. I tail him through the city and think of ways to mess with his car. Cut his brakes or something. But I really don't know anything about cars. The Audi slows down and pulls over to the side of the road. I slow down too, not sure what he's doing. He gets out of the car and walks back towards the trunk. He leans against the back of the car and I ride up to him slowly.

"Having fun, Romeo?" he asks.

"What do you mean?" I ask.

"You know what I mean. Are you having fun screwing my wife?"

Adrenaline shoots through me and I want to hit him. He has a smirk on his face a mile long.

"She thinks you're an asshole," I say.

He grabs my shirt at the neck and my bike clatters to the ground.

"We call you Romeo, you know. She tells me everything."

"No she doesn't."

"Sure she does. She tells me all the details. How you have sex. What you say. What you say before you come."

He lets go of my shirt and I fall back over my bike on the ground. My hand comes down on the spokes and then the pavement.

"I love you, Bunny," he says.

I get up and run at him, pushing his chest with all my strength. He stumbles back against the trunk of the car and then grabs me and pins me to the ground. He punches me in the face. I can taste blood and I'm crying, which pisses me off.

"She doesn't love you," I yell at him.

He bashes the back of my head into the pavement a few times.

"Don't be a fucking punk," he says and holds his fist above my face. "You're living in a fucking dream world. We were using you. Lick your wounds and get over it." He gets off me and steps back.

I roll onto my side. My head feels like a piano landed on it.

"Go home, Romeo," he says. "It's over."

"Did she really tell you everything?" I ask.

"Every sad little detail," he says and goes back to the car.

I go home and clean the blood off my face and try to call Karen a few times, but she doesn't answer. I leave messages telling her I love her and that it's not too late, that I would still take her back. I go out with Eric that night and we end up at the Roxy. I get blind drunk and blab all my troubles to him. He tells me to forget the bitch. I can't forget her, I tell him. Whatever, he says and starts hitting on some redhead. I end up dancing with some chick named Jill. I take her home and we start to get it on, but I feel all the booze in my gut and have to go throw up. She's sitting up in the bed when I get back, looking not too impressed, but I don't care.

"What's wrong?" she says.

"Nothing," I say. "Drank too much."

"Your pal said you were going through a breakup."

"What does he know?" I want this chick out of

my place. If I had a car I would go over to Karen's and call her out from the street. Embarrass her in front of the whole neighbourhood. Jill decides to go, and I'm glad to see her head out the door. I sit up for a bit and think of Karen. I could have been good with the kids. The next day I lay low and stay inside. I feel like shit. In the evening I'm making some soup when there is a knock at the door and I find Karen standing in the hall. For some reason seeing her makes me angry.

"What?" I say.

"Hear me out," she says. "Can I come in?"

I hold off a bit, let her suffer in my silence, and then stand aside. She comes in and leans up against the arm of the couch, just like the first time she came into my apartment.

"Sorry," she says. "I didn't mean for things to go this far."

"What did you mean to happen?" I ask.

"I don't know," she says.

She tells me it's her husband's deal and that she just stuck around with me because she was bored and because she could.

"That doesn't help my feelings," I say.

"Screw your feelings," she says. "What are you, nineteen?"

"Twenty," I say.

"You don't know what your feelings are."

"I do," I say. "I know I love you."

"Well, too bad," she says.

"Why are you being such a bitch?"

"None of this is going to matter," she says. "In a few years you'll be elsewhere, with different people. None of this shit matters."

"And what about you?" I ask. "Where will you be?" I go up to her and start kissing her neck. At first she pushes me away, but I fight back. I know this is our last time.

THE FILM DIRECTOR AND THE PIXIE

In his hotel room, the director took a mouthful of Scotch, swallowed a Viagra, and then headed off to the gala. He pushed past women with diamonds around their necks and stiletto heels under their manicured feet. At the bar he ordered another Scotch and fiddled with the gold links on his French cuffs. Men gathered in corners were discussing fishing trips to Chile and starlets they had bedded. The director grabbed two cubes of blue cheese from the tray of a passing waiter. He considered his cholesterol level, ate the cheese, and then wiped his meaty lips with rough swipes of a cocktail napkin.

A pixie with a broken wing and limbs like a fawn leaned in against the bar beside him and ordered a glass of Chablis. The director swirled the Scotch in his glass and said, you look like a young Mia Farrow. The pixie adjusted the ankle strap on her Miu Miu heels. Does that line usually work? she asked, crinkling her nose. He held out a business card and said, I could make you famous. Wow, she said, and sipped from her wine glass, I don't care if I'm famous. He stuffed the card back into his pocket. Everyone wants to be famous, he said. The pixie shrugged her shoulders and surveyed the room. I think I could love you, the director said. He took her hand. The pixie lit a cigarette. Do you think I want your love? she asked. He leaned in close to her. You're a tiger, he said, just like my first wife.

They went out on to the cobbled street and down a lane to a path that led into the woods. Their breath left frosty wisps in the air. They came to a clearing near a half-frozen pond. Are you in love? the pixie asked, and touched him on the mouth. Then she loosened his tie. I'm always in love, he said, and cupped her breasts in his hands. Her dress slipped down over her hips and gathered on the snow around her feet. What do you want? she asked. The director unfastened his belt. Everything, he said. Snow-flakes drifted from the sky and melted on their skin. A deer stepped into the clearing and held still for a moment before it turned and darted back into the woods. I want to start over, he said. His heart beat fast and hard in his ears. Whisky jacks in the trees nuzzled their heads into their breasts and turned their backs. The cold burned the director's hands and face. He tasted the pixie's fingers and kissed her neck. He would take her home, marry her, and give her credit cards with no limit. The pixie's flesh grew warm and a blue light suffused the air around them. The direc-tor remembered the time he touched Phoebe Daw-son in the back of his father's Pontiac. I love you, he said. The pixie laughed and stirred the snow from the branches of trees.

In the morning the director woke against a snowdrift under a pine tree. His tie was gone, his shirt ripped. He pushed himself up and crunched through fresh snow to the hotel. In the lobby he caught his reflec-tion in a mirrored pillar. His face was smooth, his hair dark and glossy. He ran his hands over his taut, flat stomach. I'm young, he said, I'm young. He went up to his room, but his key card wouldn't work in the door. At the reception desk they said they didn't have a room in his name. That's impossible, he said, and banged his fist on the counter. He hitched up his pants, which were now several sizes too large for him, and went into the street. The wind whipped up under his jacket and chilled his skin. He stuffed his hands into his empty pockets.

NOT THE RIGHT THINGS

The sound of a chainsaw from somewhere in the neighbourhood wakes Brian, and he sits up and finds that Crystal is not beside him.

"Christ," he says and drops back against the pillows. She'll be in the spare room again, painting the walls. He would have liked a simple morning, waking and holding his wife. At one time they would stay in bed all day enjoying each other. He closes his eyes and slips a hand under the waistband of his pyjama bottoms and cups his partial erection.

Last night, they were driving home and he thought of taking the chance, with just the two of them in the car, of broaching the subject of what might be happening to their relationship. He was about to say what was on his mind when a car pulled out in front of them from a hidden driveway. He slammed on the brakes and punched the horn. Crystal's arm shot out and braced against the dashboard.

"Watch where you're going," she said.

"I was," Brian said. "The guy came from nowhere." Instantly he wanted to take it back, loathing the whiney tone in his own voice. For the rest of the drive home Crystal said nothing. He longed for her to say something kind. At home, Crystal went to the kitchen and Brian to the bedroom. He waited to hear her footsteps on the stairs, wanting her to come to bed. Before he turned out the light, the thought occurred to him that some invisible line had been crossed between the two of them. And that he didn't know what that line was.

Brian pulls his hand out of his pyjamas and gets out of bed. In the hall, near the spare room, there is the familiar tearing sound of wet paint being rolled onto the walls. He goes to the garage and shoves his feet into a pair of old tennis shoes. From his toolbox he grabs a joint, then collects the morning paper from the front step. Lawns on the street have started to yellow with the summer heat and water restrictions. He pulls a deck chair onto the driveway, sits down, and lights the joint. With his lungs full of smoke he wonders what the fuck the day will bring. The morning sun warms the back of his neck.

He flips through the sports section and then checks out the rock concerts in entertainment. None of the bands are familiar to him, and he realizes he hasn't been to a concert in over seven years. His attention is pulled away when the neighbour's sixteen-year-old son Trevor pulls his 1964 midnight-blue Chevy Malibu into the driveway on the other side of the hedge. Trevor revs the engine a few times before cutting the ignition and getting out of the car.

"Just getting in?" Brian calls out.

"Yup," Trevor says.

Lucky bugger, Brian thinks and gets up. He skirts around the hedge and joins Trevor beside the Malibu. He runs his hand along the paint job and asks how the car's been running.

"Like a dream," Trevor says. "Check out the new mags."

"Nice," Brian says. "You out with your girl? What's her name, Tammy?"

"Tammy and I broke up. It's Beth now."

"Of course," Brian says. "What did you and Beth get up to?"

"You know, Mr Pike, the usual."

"Remind me what the usual is," he says.

"We cruised around, drove up to Horth Hill, you know. Then we went over to her aunt's place. Her aunt's out of town."

"The out-of-town aunt," Brian says and glances back at the house for signs of Crystal. The siding could use a new coat of paint. "What's the sex like?" Brian says.

Trevor's face scrunches up. "I don't know," he says. "Okay, I guess."

"Is she good?"

"Sure, better than Tammy."

"Well, that's great." Brian pats the car and glances one more time at the house and shades his eyes against the sun. He considers pressing for more detail but worries about appearing to be a creep. "Do you love her?"

"Who? Beth?" Trevor asks.

"Sure, Beth," Brian says.

"Man, I don't know."

"The car?" Brian asks.

"More than anything, Mr Pike."

When Brian goes back into the house he finds the spare room empty and the walls wet with dark pink paint. A drop sheet covers the crib in the corner. We need to go to Mexico, he thinks. Some sun and sand. And then another thought, a recurring thought, comes to him of going on a road trip but not with Crystal. Going by himself, driving down through Montana, the Dakotas, Kansas. Cheap hotels and dingy taverns with neon Budweiser signs in the windows. He goes to the kitchen where Crystal stands at the stove scrambling eggs in a frying pan. She's wearing a pair of khaki-coloured shorts that he finds particularly nice on her ass and a blue T-shirt.

"Are you going to get dressed today?" she asks.

He smoothes a hand down the front of his T-shirt. "Do I have to?"

"Yes, the candle party is tonight."

"Don't we have enough candles?"

She scrapes the eggs onto a plate and puts the frying pan and spatula into the dishwasher. "Bonding with Trevor?" she asks.

"He got new mags."

"Great."

He hates her sarcastic tone.

"What? I can't talk with the neighbour's kid?"

Crystal takes her plate, slides the patio door open,

and steps out onto the deck. As Brian catches her gaze, she frowns and slides the door closed.

"Jesus," Brian says and takes a few steps toward her and then changes his mind and goes up to the bedroom to get dressed.

Before anyone arrives for the candle party, Brian drives over to the Sail & Mast for a couple of beer and a few games of pool. When last call is announced, he's surprised that he's still there and stumbles out into the parking lot unable to remember where he parked the truck. He considers the idea that he might have walked to the pub and decides to call a cab. Then on the way to the pay phone he comes across his truck and pulls out his keys and takes a stab at the lock. The keys clatter to the ground. He kneels down and bashes his head into the door panel. Someone calls out, "Mr Pike," and Brian straightens up to find that Trevor has pulled up in the Malibu.

"Looks like you're having trouble," Trevor says.

Brian guesses that the pale blonde girl sitting in the passenger seat is Beth. In the back there is a girl with short black hair and heavy eye makeup. She waves and smiles.

"I've had a bit to drink," Brian says and slips the

keys back into his pocket. "Maybe you'd help an old man out and give me a lift home?"

The passenger-side door swings opens and the front seat pulls forward, allowing Brian to crawl into the back. The girl with the eye makeup offers him a beer.

"What are you guys up to?" Brian asks.

"Going to the park to smoke up," Trevor says.

"That sounds good right now," Brian says. "Let's go."

They take the highway toward the ferry terminal and exit onto an empty street that leads them to a gravel loop of forested campsites. Trevor pulls the car into a vacant site where a picnic table and fire pit appear in the headlights just before Trevor switches off and blackness surrounds them. Trevor takes a joint from the visor. Brian opens another beer and waits.

"Is this where you hang out?" Brian asks.

"Here or Horth Hill," the girl with the eye makeup says and tells him her name is Rebecca.

She pinches the joint between thumb and forefinger and takes a long drag before passing it on. She pops open a beer and leans back against the side panel. She kicks Brian in the calf with the pointed toe of her shoe. "How old are you?" she asks.

He's about to say thirty-two but then stops himself. He hasn't been thirty-two in years, but for some reason that's the age that pops into his mind. "Thirty-seven," he says.

"Cool," she says and leans toward him. "Do you have a house and stuff?"

"Shut up, Beck," Trevor says. "He's my neighbour."

Rebecca leans back again and takes out a pack of gum. She drops two white tablets into her mouth and holds out the pack for Brian.

"Are you married?" she asks.

Brian opens his mouth to say something, but Trevor jumps in. "Yes, he's married. He has a car, a house, a yard."

"All right," Rebecca says. "No need to be an ass." She leans toward Brian and touches his thigh. "Just curious."

Axl Rose singing "Sweet Child o' Mine" booms from the speakers. Brian rests his head against the window, grateful for the thorough numbness of his body. Outside only the slightest outlines of tree trunks mark the darkness. He hopes Crystal is cheating on him and for a moment pictures her with other men. His wife in the back seat of her red Passat with some guy he doesn't know. Damp hair and skin. He decides to forgive her.

They leave the park, drive past the high school, and stop in front of a white-stucco bungalow. Rebecca taps Brian on the knee.

"'Bye," she says and jumps out of the car. She runs across the lawn and waves just before she opens the door and steps into the house. They pull away from the curb, and Brian knows there'll be no way to explain to Crystal what he has been up to. In front of Beth's house, Trevor asks if Brian wants to come in for a drink. He considers walking home to get some of the booze and dope out of his system, but follows Beth and Trevor through Beth's front door and into her living room.

"You like scotch?" she asks, and without waiting for an answer pours liquid from a crystal decanter into two glasses. She hands one to Brian and takes a sip of the other before passing it to Trevor.

"Won't your father notice booze missing?" Brian asks.

Beth shrugs her shoulders. "He's never said anything."

Wow, he thinks. That's pretty cool, and he wonders if he could be like that with his kids, laid back, not stressing. If there are children, and he realizes he has never really thought about it one way or the other. Guys at work talk about their kids, and he never has any other emotion than detached disinterest. Yet when he's with Trevor and Beth, he wants to know what they will say next. This leads him to contemplate what might come out of the mouths of his own children. Would his own son be like Trevor? Beth drops down onto the couch and kicks one long bare leg out over the other. The star tattooed on her ankle blips back and forth along with her toenails painted a bright golden yellow. Brian jolts forward. He has been gawking at her calves and feet.

"I have to go," he says and puts the glass on the coffee table. When he stands his knee buckles, and he braces himself with the arm of the couch.

Trevor asks if he can drive him home, but Brian says he needs the air and makes a hasty exit.

Out on the street, he starts to run until the heaving pain in his chest causes him to stagger. Why don't I run anymore? he asks himself. He has to start eating healthy food again. Tomorrow he'll set up the weights in the garage.

Brian can see from the street that there are no lights on in his house. He lets himself in through the basement and goes upstairs to the bedroom and finds the bed empty. He goes from room to room until he comes across Crystal asleep on the couch in the TV room. He kneels at her side. Her face is slack and he wants to touch her cheek or her mouth but is afraid he will wake her. This beautiful face, he thinks, why can it be so evil?

"I don't know what I'm doing," he says and picks at the carpet.

"Good night," he says. "I love you," he adds and goes upstairs.

In the morning Brian wakes up with a headache. He gets ready for work and decides not to check in on Crystal before he walks into town, grabs his truck, and drives to the job site. He figures he'll give her a call before lunch. Test the waters.

Later in the day, he grabs a break and calls home, but there is no answer. She must be out shopping, he guesses, and tries her a few hours later. When she doesn't pick up he starts to call every hour until he leaves the site at the end of the day. He gets home and her car is gone and for a moment a vision flashes in his mind of finding the house empty. All of Crystal's things gone, even the furniture and dishes. He runs up the stairs and is relieved that the living room is unchanged. In the bedroom the drawers and closet are still full of Crystal's clothes. He picks her lime-green cardigan off the bed and studies the label. Dry clean only. She can't be gone, she left her things. He's sure that she will show up at any moment. He prides himself on not being like some of the guys he works with. Guys that want to know where their wives or girlfriends are at all times; guys that need to know every last detail.

He goes to the spare room. The walls are no longer pink but white and dry. The ladder is gone along with the plastic tarp that usually sits folded in a neat square on the floor in the corner. The crib is also gone. Only four indents in the carpet mark where it stood. Under the stairs he finds the crib dismantled and leaning against the wall. This is a good sign, he thinks. Now maybe she'll relax and they can treat each other like they used to. He is elevated by the thought and gets the idea that they should go to the pool tonight. It has been a long time, maybe a year or two, since they have gone to the pool. They used to go at least once a week. He decides to make dinner and then suggest they go swimming. In the kitchen he opens the fridge and pulls out pork chops and salad mixings and sets them out on the counter. He goes to the living room and turns up the Def Leppard CD in the stereo.

He is pulling hot, foil-wrapped potatoes from the oven when he notices that it is almost eight o'clock. He calls Crystal's cell and still there is no answer. He thinks to call her mother's place but then remembers she is in Egypt. He decides to call the house anyway. The phone rings, but there is no answering machine. He turns the music off and goes to the front window and watches for her car to turn into the cul-de-sac. In the kitchen he takes a sheet of paper from one of the drawers and writes a note. "I have gone out looking for you. If you are reading this stay put. I will be home soon." He gets in the truck and drives through the downtown streets, past the yellow glow of the Dairy Queen, the Shoppers Drug Mart, the Safeway. He peeks into the light behind the windows and tries to spot his wife. He drives down near the new developments on the harbour and then up toward the airport. For old times' sake he decides to head out to Ardmore where he used to hang in high school. He turns into a side street and comes across a few parked cars. One of them is Trevor's. He can't believe this is still where the kids go. Nothing changes in this town. He parks and walks over to Trevor's car and knocks on the driver's window. Trevor rolls the window down and releases a cascade of pot smoke.

"Hey, man," Trevor says. "You freaked me out."

"Can I join you?" Brian says and jogs around to the passenger side and gets in. "You by yourself?" Brian says.

Trevor points at another car and says that Beth is over there. He lights a joint, takes a toke, and passes it over to Brian. They sit in silence and smoke.

"Why you out here, Mr Pike?" Trevor asks.

Brian shakes his head.

"I don't know," he says and almost starts to laugh. There are too many distracting things in this car, he thinks. He pushes the door lock down and then thinks differently and pulls it up. "This is where we used to hang out." There is a long stream of silence and then Brian says, "I was looking for my wife."

"Would she be here?"

"No," Brian says. "I don't know where she would be."

"That sucks," Trevor says and carves the letter 'S' in the condensation on the window, sending a trickle of water to slip down the glass to the ledge.

Brian holds his face in his hands for a moment. "I don't know my wife," he says. "All these years, to be with someone and know nothing about them. Absolutely nothing."

"You must know something about her," Trevor says.

"Not the right things," Brian says. "I know only the wrong things."

Trevor starts to laugh and his laugh turns into a hacking cough. "I know the wrong things about people too."

Brian puts a hand on Trevor's shoulder. "You're a good kid. If I had a son I would want him to be like you."

"Thanks, Mr Pike," Trevor says.

"I got to go," Brian says and gets out of the car. He stumbles back to the truck. He's sure the pot is stronger than it was when he was in high school. On the drive toward home he criss-crosses the neighbourhood hoping to see Crystal walking home or her car parked in some driveway. He pulls the truck up in front of their house and goes straight to the kitchen where he calls 9-1-1 and tells the operator that his wife is missing.

"How long has she been gone?" the operator asks.

"Maybe sixteen hours," he says.

She asks him a series of questions that he can only answer no to. Do you know what she was wearing? Do you know where she might have gone? Did she take any belongings? Are there items missing from the house? Are there any signs of a struggle?

The operator tells him they will send over officers, when they have a chance, to fill out a full report. She adds that they need to wait for twenty-four hours before they can officially start a search.

"She's never done this," he says.

"Was there an argument?"

"Maybe," Brian says. "I don't know."

After he hangs up the phone he goes to the spare room. Maybe there is something there he missed. A clue to his wife's whereabouts. But again he is only met with white walls and an empty room. Why white? He wonders what the white is called: bright white, perfect white, snow white. Does it mean something? He presses his hand over the faint indent of a crib leg in the carpet. Why put the crib away? When he leaves the room, he turns the light off and shuts the door. He goes down the hall to the unlit living room and sits in the La-Z-Boy. He thinks of the things he does know about Crystal. He knows she loves to swim in the ocean. She loves oak trees. But why? This is what he realizes he doesn't know.

There is a flash of light on the wall from a car turning into the cul-de-sac. He goes to the window, but it is only Trevor coming home. The light fills the room for a moment and then turns in on itself and is gone.

FATTY

We watched Fatty for a while, sure he had been in the neighbourhood all his life, but that's no excuse for the disgusting bulk he carried around, it's no reason for us not to want him dead or at least to ask him to move. At first we left notes under the windshield wiper of his Toyota. Nothing very threatening, just stuff like, get out fat pig we want you gone. But zilch happened. We still had to see him waddle from his house every morning and get into that pathetically small car and drive off to wherever he worked. And then be assaulted again in the evening by his freak-show girth.

Judy was in Safeway and saw him in the cereal aisle buying Captain Crunch. Like, who eats that crap, and he's an adult. No example to our children at all.

Our children have never eaten wheat, milk, meat, or sugar. Judy had little Tyler with her and Tyler tugged on her sleeve and asked, Mom, why is that man so fat? Terrible to have to expose a child to such a thing.

Nobody ever stopped by his place. Imagine, no visitors except for the pizza guy. God knows his family had probably stopped talking to him. We made Carl, Ginger's husband, go over there and tell him how we felt. Of course, we shouldn't have left anything up to Carl. He would never have even made it through medical school if Ginger hadn't been there to hold his hand every moment of the day. How does she put up with him? When Carl came back, we all gathered around him and asked what it was like inside Fatty's hovel. Carl said it was nice. Nice! Christ, that's a good one. He said it was clean and he had a picture on the wall of Algonquin Provincial Park. This made us laugh, what would Fatty know about being outside? The man couldn't have hiked a day in his life. So we asked Carl, is he leaving? Carl shrugged his measly shoulders and said, don't know. Useless, absolutely useless. So the other night we're all together, and Carol starts to get really worked up about Fatty being in the neighbourhood. We had had a few glasses of wine and wrote a note telling him he would have to leave or we were going to chase him out and that we were going to tell the police he downloaded child porn. Which we were all sure he was doing anyway. No wife and all. God knows what deviant crap he got up to. So we tied the note to a brick and tossed it through his front window. We laughed all night about that.

We were just not having any effect. We would still see him as usual, pulling his fat ass in and out of his car. The front window of his house was replaced. On the weekend he would be in his backyard mowing the lawn or trimming the hedges. We just couldn't have it. We knocked on his door one evening after dinner. He opened the door and smiled at us and asked if anything was the matter. Helen pushed passed him and said, you bet. He stepped back and let us all in. Don't you think you would feel more comfortable living somewhere else, Judy asked, somewhere where there are others like you? His chubby hands fell to his side and his big yap dropped open. Carol pointed her finger at him, it's disgusting, she said, what about our children? He seemed to have nothing to say. His face went blotchy. The TV murmured behind us. There was the smell of dust and Pine-Sol. I've lived here all my life, he said, I went to school here, I grew up here. Fran, who is prone to emotional meltdowns and Ativan binges, especially since her son went to college and decided he was gay, picked up a vase that was on the table beside the door and smashed it across his head. He covered his head with his arms to shield himself. There were shards of ceramic all over the carpet. There was blood, but we couldn't tell from where. Helen hit him on the back, and Ginger kicked him between the legs. His knees buckled, and he fell to the ground.

From behind the silk drapes of our houses, we watched the police and the coroner show up a few days later. Yellow tape went up. There was a small article in the paper; no motive and no suspects, a possible home invasion. A For Sale sign was placed on the front lawn.

We never spoke of the incident, and over time we thought about it less and less.

THE PLUM PIT

At lunchtime the CEO left the office and strolled into the downtown bustle. He bought a plum from a street vendor and found a seat on a bench in a green space wedged between two office buildings. He pulled at the collar of his shirt and loosened his tie. Women walked by in business skirts and high-heeled shoes. The CEO bit into the plum and slumped his shoulders. Bus brakes squealed, horns honked. He pushed the last bit of plum into his mouth and sucked the pulpy flesh from the pit. A fire engine sped past with sirens wailing. The CEO swallowed the last bit of plum and pain flashed across his neck. The pit lodged in his throat. He lurched up and stumbled. There was no one around. He tried to force air out of his lungs and beat his chest with his fists. His vision flickered. He stumbled to the side and then threw himself chest first against the bench. The pit shifted and slipped down his throat. Air rushed in and out of his lungs.

In the office the CEO put his belongings in a cardboard box. The gold pen, the certificates. A cramp pinched his side and he sat down. What of the pit? he thought. He sent an email to the employees. This place is a prison, it said, you dream of the outside, but you fear you'll fumble in the fresh air. He left the box on his desk and went home to his penthouse. He stirred a gin and tonic. What if I had died? There was no wife, no children. He had a brother he hadn't seen in twelve years. What of the pit? he asked himself and opened the sliding-glass door to the balcony, letting in the sounds of the city. Why did I think I would be different?

The next morning he slept in and spent the day in his undershirt and shorts. He went through his photographs, pulled his suits and ties from the closet, and dropped them down the garbage chute. His assistant called and asked if he was all right. I'm turning into a tree, he said. The assistant went silent. The CEO hung up the phone and pulled the cord from the wall. Pain blinked in his chest.

At a garden store the CEO bought a big clay pot, potting soil, and fish fertilizer. He carried the pot out onto his deck, filled it with soil, and then drank the bottle of fertilizer. He remembered stories his grandmother had told him when he was a child about how the trees came alive at night and roamed the earth. Sharp pains popped in his arms and legs. He wondered if he should stand in the pot of soil now or wait till roots pushed through the soles of his feet. He took his shoes off and then his pants and shirt. There was the hum of city traffic below. He sat in a deck chair and waited for branches to poke through his chest. He imagined the leaves that would bud from young branches.

PLEASE COME BACK

A few days ago Brad's big toe, the last toe he has left, started to talk to him. On the bus the toe says, hey loser, you look like a slob. At night the toe wakes him with a deep throbbing that travels up his leg and into his hips. Nobody loves you, the toe says. You're dirt. You're a shit-head, loser. He kicks the toe against the bedpost and covers his head with the pillow. Shut up, shut up, he cries. But the toe is loud, and Brad knows it's right.

Brad calls Stacy every hour. I love you, please come back, he says to her voicemail. One day he went home and her clothes were gone. She left behind the stuffed animals Brad had bought for her, even the one that he gave her on their first date, the two panda bears hugging.

He cut off the first toe when he was nine, with a Swiss Army knife, out in the wooded area behind his house. His dad had been missing for over a week. His mom was staying in bed all day and told Brad to beat it when he opened the door to her room. She would get up every once in a while and make toast or a martini. He asked her where dad was, but all she did was stare past him with glazed eyes. He left because you're stupid and ugly, Brad's little toe said. Because you suck at bowling. Because you're trash.

Stacy tells Brad they will never be together again and that he has things he needs to work out on his own. Brad can't believe that what she says is true, although the toe says it is.

All day at the record store where Brad works, not one person comes in. People pass by the front windows, couples arm in arm, children with their parents, and no one even looks his way. Something about it makes him so damn sad. He calls Stacy, but she doesn't an-swer. He walks home through the rain. You're never going to be anything, the toe says. You'll die alone and nobody will come to your funeral. Brad starts to cry. People cross the street to avoid him. He wipes his nose on his T-shirt. Pussy boy, the toe says. In the lobby of his apartment building, Brad yells, shut up, shut up, at the toe. But the toe gets louder and he runs up to his apartment and digs through a kitchen drawer for a cleaver. He tosses his wet runners aside, peels off his sock, and silences the toe with one swift chop. A bright light overwhelms him, and there is a silence so empty he can hear the particles in the air chafing.

He wraps the toe in a paper towel, puts it in the fridge, and then sits on the floor and holds his throbbing foot with both hands. The fridge makes a drip-drip sound and then sets into a loud steady hum. He wishes Stacy was there, making him grilled cheese sandwiches and Jell-O. He opens the fridge and picks up the bundle of white paper towel. Inside where the severed toe was there is now a black pearl. He rolls the pearl around in his palm and then puts it in his mouth and swallows. He straightens his back and puffs out his chest. He wants to run along a beach, smell the ocean air. He feels worthy of love, of affection. He picks up the phone and dials Stacy's number.

RHONDA WATERFALL was born in 1973 in Ocean Falls, BC. She studied creative writing with the Writer's Studio at Simon Fraser University. Her work has appeared in *Geist, Descant,* and several other literary journals. *The Only Thing I Have* is her first book. She currently lives and works in Vancouver.